SUGAR CREEK GANG
The WATERMELON MYSTERY

Paul Hutchens

MOODY PRESS
CHICAGO

All Scripture quotations are taken from the *New American Standard Bible*, © 1960, 1962, 1963, 1968, 1971, 1972, 1973, 1975, 1977, and 1994 by The Lockman Foundation, La Habra, Calif. Used by permission.

ISBN: 0-8024-7032-7

1 3 5 7 9 10 8 6 4 2

Printed in the United States of America

PREFACE

Hi—from a member of the Sugar Creek Gang!

It's just that I don't know which one I am. When I was good, I was Little Jim. When I did bad things—well, sometimes I was Bill Collins or even mischievous Poetry.

You see, I am the daughter of Paul Hutchens, and I spent many an hour listening to him read his manuscript as far as he had written it that particular day. I went along to the north woods of Minnesota, to Colorado, and to the various other places he would go to find something different for the Gang to do.

Now the years have passed—more than fifty, actually. My father is in heaven, but the Gang goes on. All thirty-six books are still in print and now are being updated for today's readers with input from my five children, who also span the decades from the '50s to the '70s.

The real Sugar Creek is in Indiana, and my father and his six brothers were the original Gang. But the idea of the books and their ministry were and are the Lord's. It is He who keeps the Gang going.

PAULINE HUTCHENS WILSON

1

If I hadn't been so proud of the prize water-melon I had grown from the packet of special seed Dad had ordered from the state experiment station, maybe I wouldn't have been so fighting mad when somebody sneaked into our garden that summer night and stole it.

I was not only proud of that beautiful, oblong, dark green melon, but I was going to save the seed for planting next year. I was, in fact, planning to go into the watermelon-raising business.

Dad and I had had the soil of our garden tested, and it was just right for melons, which means it was well-drained, well-ventilated, and with plenty of natural plant food. We would never have to worry about moisture in case there would ever be a dry summer, because we could carry water from the iron pitcher pump that was just inside the south fence. Our family had another pitcher pump not more than fifteen feet from the back door of our house. Both pumps got mixed up in the mystery of the stolen watermelon, which I'm going to tell you about right now.

Mom and I were down in the watermelon patch one hot day that summer, looking around a little, admiring my melon, and guessing how many seeds she might have buried in her nice red inside.

"Let's give her a name," I said to Mom. The Collins family, which is ours, gives names to nearly every living thing around our farm anyway.

She answered, "All right. Let's call her Ida."

Mom caught hold of the pump handle and pumped it up and down quite a few fast, squeaking times to fill the pail I was holding under the spout.

"Why Ida?" I asked with a grunt, as the pail was getting heavier with every stroke of the pump handle.

Mom's answer sounded sensible. "Ida means 'thirsty.' I noticed it yesterday when I was looking through a book of names for babies."

I had never seen such a thirsty melon in all my life. Again and again, day after day, I carried water to her, pouring it into the circular trough I had made in the ground around the roots of the vine she was growing on. And always the next morning, the water would be gone. Knowing a watermelon is more than 92 percent water anyway, I knew if she kept on taking water like that, she'd get to be one of the fattest melons in the whole Sugar Creek territory.

Mom and I threaded our way through the open spaces between the vines, dodging a lot of smaller melons grown from ordinary seed, till we came to the little trough that circled Ida's vine. While I was emptying my pail of water into it, I said, "OK, Ida, my girl. That's your name: *Ida Watermelon Collins*. How do you like it?"

I stooped, snapped my third finger several times against her fat green side, and called her by name again, saying, "By this time next year you'll be the mother of a hundred other melons. And year after next, you'll be the grandmother of more melons than you can shake a stick at."

I sighed a long, noisy, happy sigh, thinking about what a wonderful summer day it was and how good it felt to be alive—to be a boy and to live in a boy's world.

I carried another pail of water, poured it into Ida's trough, and then stopped to rest in the shade of the elderberry bushes near the fence. Dad and I had put up a brand-new woven wire fence there early in the spring, and at the top of it we had stretched two strands of barbed wire, making it dangerous for anybody to climb over the fence in a hurry. In fact, the only place anybody would be able to get over *really* fast would be at the stile we were going to build near the pitcher pump, halfway between the pump and the elderberry bushes.

We would *have* to get the stile built pretty soon, I thought. In another few weeks school would start, and I would want to do as I'd always done—go through or over the fence there to get to the lane, which was a shortcut to school.

I didn't have the slightest idea then that somebody would try to steal my melon or that the stealing of it would plunge me into the exciting middle of one of the most dangerous mysteries there had ever been in the Sugar Creek territory. Most certainly I never dreamed that Ida Watermelon Collins would have a share in helping the Sugar Creek Gang capture a fugitive from justice, an actual runaway thief the police had been looking for for quite a while.

We found out about the thief one hot summer night about a week later, when Poetry, the barrel-shaped member of our gang, stayed all night with me in his green tent, which my parents had let us pitch under the spreading branches of the plum tree in our yard.

Of course, everything didn't happen that very first night, but *one* of the most exciting and confusing things did. It wouldn't have happened, though, if we hadn't gotten out of our cots and started on a pajama-clad hike in the moonlight down through the woods to the spring—Poetry in his green-striped pajamas and I in my red-striped ones and Dragonfly in—

But I hadn't planned to tell you just yet that Dragonfly was with us that night—which he wasn't at first. Dragonfly is the spindle-legged, pop-eyed member of our gang. He is always showing up when we don't need him or want him and when we least expect him and is always getting us into trouble—or else we have to help get him *out* of trouble.

Now that I've mentioned Dragonfly and

hinted that he was the cause of some of our trouble—mine especially—I'd better tell you that he and I had the same kind of red-striped pajamas. Our mothers had seen the same ad in the *Sugar Creek Times* and had gone shopping the same afternoon in the same Sugar Creek Dry Goods Store and had seen the same bargains in boys' nightclothes—two pairs of red-striped pajamas being the only kind left when they got there.

Little Tom Till's mother—Tom was the newest member of our gang—had seen the ad about the sale, too, and his mother and mine had bought for their two red-haired, freckle-faced sons blue denim jeans exactly alike and maroon-and-gray-striped T-shirts exactly alike. When Tom and I were together anywhere, you could hardly tell us apart. So I looked like Little Tom Till in the daytime and like Dragonfly at night.

Poor Dragonfly! All the gang felt very sorry for him because he not only is very spindle-legged and pop-eyed, but in ragweed season—which it was at that time of the year—his crooked nose, which turns south at the end, is always sneezing, and also he gets asthma.

Before I get into the middle of the stolen watermelon story, I'd better explain that my wonderful grayish brown haired mother had been having what is called "insomnia" that summer. So Dad had arranged for her to sleep upstairs in our guest bedroom. That was the farthest away from the night noises of our farm, especially the ones that came from the direction of the barn. Mom simply had to have her rest, or she wouldn't be able to keep on doing all the things a farm mother has to do every day all summer.

That guest room was also the farthest away from the tent under the plum tree—which Poetry and I decided maybe was another reason that Dad had put Mom upstairs.

Just one other thing I have to explain quick is that the reason Poetry was staying at my house for a week was that his parents were on a vacation in Canada and had left Poetry with us. He and I were going to have a vacation at the same time by sleeping in his tent in our yard.

It was a *very* hot late summer night, the time of year when the cicadas were as much a part of a Sugar Creek night as sunshine is part of the day. Cicadas are broad-headed, protruding-eyed insects, which some people call locusts and others call harvest flies. In the late summer evenings, they set the whole country half crazy with their whirring sounds from the trees, where thousands of them are like an orchestra with that many members, each member playing nothing but a drum.

I was lying on my hot cot just across the tent from Poetry in his own hot cot, each of us having tried about seven times to go to sleep, which Dad had ordered us to do about seventy times seven times that very night, barking out his orders from the back door or from the living-room window.

Poetry, being in a mischievous mood, was right in the middle of quoting one of his favorite poems, "The Village Blacksmith," speaking to an imaginary audience out in the barnyard, when Dad called to us again to keep still. His voice came bellowing out through the drumming of the cicadas, saying, "Bill Collins, if you boys don't stop talking and laughing and go to *sleep,* I'm coming out there and *put* you to sleep!"

A few seconds later, he added in a still-thundery voice, "I've told you boys for the last time! You're keeping Charlotte Ann awake—and you're liable to wake up your mother too!" When Dad says anything like that, I know he really means it, especially when he has already said it *that* many times.

I knew it was no time of night for my cute little brown-haired sister, Charlotte Ann, to be awake, and certainly my nice friendly-faced mother would need a lot of extra sleep, because tomorrow was Saturday and there would be the house to clean, pies and cookies to bake for Sunday, and a million chores a farm woman has to do every Saturday.

"Wonderful!" Poetry whispered across to me. "He won't tell us anymore. He's told us for the last time. We can laugh and talk now as much as we want to!"

"You don't know Dad," I said.

"I'm thirsty," he said. "Let's go get a drink." His voice came across the darkness like the voice of a duck with laryngitis.

Right away there was a squeaking of the springs of his cot as he rolled himself into a sitting position. He swung his feet out of bed and set them *ker-plop* on the canvas floor of the tent. I could see him sitting there like the shadow of a fat grizzly in the moonlight that filtered in through the plastic net window just above my cot.

A split second later, he was across the three feet of space between us and sitting on the edge of *my* cot, making it groan almost loud enough for Dad to hear.

"Let's go!" he said, using a businesslike tone.

I certainly didn't want to get up and go with him to get a drink. Besides, I knew that the very minute we started to pump the iron pitcher pump at the end of the board walk, not more than fifteen feet from our kitchen door, Dad would hear the pump pumping and the water splashing into the big iron kettle under the spout. He would come storming out, with or without words, and would start saying again something he had already said for the last time.

I yawned the laziest, longest yawn I could, sighed the longest, drawn-out sigh I could, and said to Poetry, "I'm too sleepy. You go and get a drink for *both* of us."

Then I sighed once more, turned over, and began to breathe heavily, as though I was sound asleep.

But Poetry couldn't be stopped by sighs and yawns. He shook me awake and said, "Come on, treat a guest with a little politeness, will you?"

He meant I had to wake up and get up and

go out with him to pump a noisy pump and run the risk of stirring up Dad's already stirred-up temper.

When I kept on breathing like a sleeping baby, Poetry said with a disgruntled grunt, "Give me one little reason why you won't help me get a drink!"

"One little reason?" I yawned up at his shadow. "I'll give you a *big* one—five feet eleven inches tall, one hundred seventy-two pounds, bushy-eyebrowed, reddish brown mustached—"

"You want me to die of thirst?" asked Poetry.

"Thirst or whatever you want to do it of. But hurry up and do it and get it over with, because I'm going to sleep."

That must have stirred up Poetry's own temper a little, because he said, "OK, pal, I'll go by myself!"

Quicker than a firefly's fleeting flash, he had zipped open the plastic screen door of the tent, whipped the canvas flap aside, and stepped out into the moonlight.

I was up and out and after him in a nervous hurry. I grabbed him by the sleeve of his green-striped pajamas.

But he wouldn't stay stopped. He growled at me and whispered, "If you try to stop me, I'll scream, and you'll be in trouble."

With that he started off on the run across the moonlit yard, not toward the pump but in a different direction—toward the front gate!—saying over his shoulder, "I'm going down to the *spring* to get a drink."

That idea was even crazier, I thought, than pumping the iron pitcher pump and waking up Dad.

But you might as well try to start a balky mule as try to stop Leslie Thompson from doing what he has made up his stubborn mind he is going to do. So a minute later, the two of us were hurrying past "Theodore Collins" on our mailbox—Theodore Collins being Dad's name. Then we were across the gravel road, over the rail fence, and following the path made by barefoot boys' feet through the woods to the spring. Poetry used his flashlight every few seconds to light the way.

And that is where we ran into our mystery!

Zippety-zip-zip, swishety-swish-swish, clomp-clomp-clomp, dodge, swerve, gallop. It's nearly always one of the happiest times of my life when I am running down that little brown path to the spring, where the gang has nearly all its meetings and where so many interesting and exciting things have happened. Generally, my barefoot gallop through the woods is in the daytime, though, and I feel like a frisky young colt turned out to pasture. I had never run down that path in red-striped pajamas at night or when I was as sleepily disgruntled as I was right that minute for having to follow a not very bright barrel-shaped boy.

So when we had passed the Black Widow Stump and the linden tree and had dashed down the steep grade to the spring itself and found a dark green watermelon floating in the cement pool that Dad had built there as a reservoir for the water, it was as easy as anything for me to get fighting angry at most anything or anybody.

A watermelon there could mean only one thing—especially when right beside it was a glass fruit jar with a pound of butter in it. It meant there were *campers* somewhere nearby. And campers in the Sugar Creek woods were something that which the Sugar Creek Gang would rather have most anything else. It meant our peace and quiet would be interrupted, that we would have to wear swimsuits when we went in swimming, and we couldn't yell and scream to each other the way we liked to do.

Poetry, who was on his haunches beside the spring, surprised me by saying, "Look! It's plugged! Let's see how ripe it is!"

Before I could have stopped him even if I had thought of trying to do it, he was working the extralarge rectangular plug out of the middle of the extralarge melon's long fat side.

It was one of the prettiest watermelons I had ever seen. In fact, it was as pretty as Ida Watermelon Collins herself.

Then Poetry had the plug out and was holding it up for me to see.

Somebody had bitten off what red there had been on the end of the plug, I noticed.

Then Poetry said, "Well, what do you know! This melon's not ripe. See, it's all white inside!"

That didn't make sense. This time of year, even a watermelon that wasn't more than *half* ripe would be at least pink inside. My eyes flashed from the rectangular plug to the hole in the melon, and Poetry was right—it *was* white inside!

Then he said, "Oh, there's something *in* it! There's a ball of white *paper* or something stuffed inside it!"

I felt curiosity creeping up and down my spine and was all set for a mystery. Hardly realizing that I was trespassing on other people's property and most certainly not having a right to, even if the melon *was* in our spring, I quickly stooped and with nervous fingers pulled out the folded piece of paper. It was the kind that comes off a loaf of bread and which, at our house, I nearly always toss into the woodbox or the wastebasket unless Mom sees me first and stops me. Sometimes she wants to save the paper and use it for wrapping sandwiches for Dad's or my lunches, mine especially during the school year.

The melon *was* ripe, I noticed. The inside was a deep, dark red.

While my mind was still trying to think up a mystery, something started to happen. From up in the woods at the top of the incline there was the sound of running feet and laughing voices. There were flashlights and flickering shadows, and it sounded like a whole flock of people coming. *People!* Only these weren't boys' voices or men's voices but *girls'* voices. *Girls!* They were giggling and laughing and coming toward the base of the linden tree just above us. In another brain-whirling second they would be where they could see us, and we'd be caught.

When you are wearing a pair of red-striped pajamas and your barrel-shaped friend is wearing a pair of green-striped pajamas, and it is night, and you hear a flock of girls running in your direction, and you are half scared of girls even in the daytime, you all of a sudden forget about a plugged watermelon floating in the nice, fresh, cool water of your spring, and you look for the quickest place you can find to hide yourself!

We couldn't make a dash up either side of the incline, because that's where the girls were. And we couldn't escape in the opposite direction, because there was a barbed-wire fence there, separating us from the creek. But we had to do *something!* If it had been a gang of boys coming, we could have stood our ground and fought if we had to. But not when it was a bevy of girls. They sounded like a flock of blackbirds getting ready to fly South for the winter, except that they weren't getting ready to fly south but *north,* which was in our direction.

"Quick!" Poetry with his faster-thinking mind cried to me. "Let's beat it!" He showed me what he wanted us to do by making a dive east toward the place where I knew we could get through a board fence and on the other side of which was a path. It wound through a forest of giant ragweeds leading to Dragonfly's dad's cornfield in the direction of the Sugar Creek Gang's swimming hole.

In another jiffy I would have followed Poetry through the fence, and we would have escaped being seen. But my right bare foot, which was standing on a thin layer of slime on the cement lip of the pool where the melon was, slipped out from under me, and I felt myself going down, *down*.

I couldn't stop myself. I struggled to regain my balance and couldn't. I couldn't even fall where my mixed-up mind told me would be a better place to fall than into the pool, which would have been in a mud puddle on the other side. Suddenly, *thuddety-whammety, slip-slop-splashety*, I was half sitting and half lying in the middle of the pool of ice-cold springwater, astride that long green watermelon like a boy astride a bucking bronco at a Sugar Creek rodeo!

From above and all around and from every direction, it seemed, there sounded the voices of happy-go-lucky girls with flashlights, probably coming to get the watermelon, or the butter in the glass jar, or maybe a pail of drinking water for their camp.

2

There wasn't any sense to what I did then because of the confusion in my mixed-up mind, if I had any mind at all. But that very minute, the light of three or four—or maybe there were seventeen—flashlights dropped over the edge of the hill. And all of them at the same time splashed down upon me, hitting me in the face and all over my red-striped pajamas.

I let loose with a wild, trembling cry like a loon's eerie ghostlike quaver, loud enough to be heard as far away as the Sugar Creek bridge. I began to wave my arms wildly, to splash around in the water, and to yell to my watermelon bronco, "Giddap! Giddap! You great big green good-for-nothing bronco!"

I let out a whole series of loon calls, splashed myself off the watermelon and out of the cement pool, and made a fast, wet dash down the path to the opening in the board fence, through which Poetry had already gone. I quickly shoved myself through. A second later I was making a wild, moonlit run up the winding barefoot boys' trail through the forest of giant ragweeds toward the swimming hole, crying like a loon all the way until I knew I was out of sight of all those noisy girls.

Even as I ran, flopping along in my wet

pajamas, I had the memory of flashlights splashing in my eyes and some of the things I heard while I was going through the fence. Some of the excited words were, "Help! Help! There's a wild animal down there at the spring!" Other girls had simply screamed, the way girls do when they are scared. But one of them had shrieked an unearthly shriek, crying, "There's a *zebra* down there—*a wild zebra, taking a bath in our drinking water!*"

That, I thought, dodging my way along the path, was almost funny. In fact, sometimes a boy feels fine inside if something he has done does make a gang of girls let out an unearthly explosion of screams. Most girls scream not because they're really scared, anyway, but because they like to make people think they are.

Where, I wondered as I zigzagged along, was Poetry?

I didn't have to wonder long. By the time I was through the tall weeds and at the edge of Dragonfly's dad's cornfield, I had caught up to where he was. His flashlight beam hit me in the face as he exclaimed in his ducklike voice, "Help! Help! A zebra! A *wild zebra!*"

I stood still with my wet pajama sleeve in front of my eyes to shield them from the blinding glare of his flashlight. "It's all your fault!" I half screamed at him. "If you hadn't had the silly notion you had to have a drink!"

His voice was saucy as he said back, "What a mess you made of things—falling into that water and yelling like a banshee! Now those

Girl Scouts will tell your folks, and your father will *really* get on your case!"

"Girl Scouts?" I exclaimed to him with teeth chattering from being so cold and still all wet with springwater. Also, for some reason I didn't feel very brave and most certainly was not very happy.

"Sure," he said, "didn't you know that? A bunch of Girl Scouts have got their tents pitched up there by the papaw bushes for a week. Old Man Paddler gave them permission. They're *his* woods, you know."

And then I *was* sad. Girl Scouts were supposed to be some of the nicest people in the world—even if they were girls, I thought. What would they think of a red-haired, freckle-faced creature of some kind that was part loon and part zebra, splashing around in their drinking water, riding like a cowboy on a watermelon, and acting absolutely crazy? I would never dare show my face where any of them could see me, or some of them would remember having seen me in the light of their flashlights.

I knew that one of the very first things some of those Girl Scouts would do this week would be to come to the Collins house to buy eggs and milk and such things as sweet corn and new potatoes. They would ask my mother whose boy I was. Besides, some of them would be bound to recognize me.

"We had better get back to the tent and into bed quick, before somebody comes running up to use your telephone to call the police or the marshal or the sheriff, to tell them some wild boys have been causing a disturbance at the camp!" Poetry said.

It was a good idea even if it was a worried one, so away we went, not the way we had come but *lickety-sizzle* straight up through Dragonfly's dad's cornfield. We would swing around the east end of the bayou and back down the south side of it until we came to the fence that goes to Bumblebee Hill, we decided.

Once we got to Bumblebee Hill we would turn southwest to the place where we always went over the rail fence in front of our house. Then we would scoot across the road and past our mailbox, hoping we wouldn't wake up Theodore Collins in the Collins west bedroom, and a minute after that would be safe in our tent once more!

The very thought of safety and the security of Poetry's nice green tent under the spreading plum tree gave me a spurt of hope and put wings on my feet. I followed my lumbering barrel-shaped friend, for the moment not remembering there would be more trouble when I got home because of my very wet red-striped night-clothes.

The wind I was making as I ran was blowing against my wet eighty-nine pounds of red-haired boy, making me feel chilly all over in spite of its being such a hot night.

It was a shame not to be able to enjoy such a pretty Sugar Creek summer night. Sugar Creek nights are almost the most wonderful thing in the world. I guess there isn't anything in the whole wide world that *sounds* better than a Sugar Creek night when you are down along the creek fishing and you hear the bullfrogs bellowing in the riffles, the katydids' rasping voices calling to one another, *"Katy-did, Katy-she-did; Katy-did, Katy-she-did!"*—and the crickets singing away, vibrating their forewings together and making one of the friendliest lonesome sounds a boy ever hears. Every now and then, you can hear a screech owl too, crying *"Shay-a-a-a-a!"* like a baby loon.

Oh, there are a lot of sounds that make a boy feel good all over—such as Old Topsy, our favorite horse, in her stall crunching corn, the strange noise the chickens make in their sleep, the wind sighing through the pine trees along the bayou, and every now and then somebody's rooster turning loose a *"Cock-a-doodle-doo!"* as if he's so proud of himself he can't wait until morning to let all the sleeping hens know about it—all as though it was a waste of good time to sleep when you could listen to such nice noisy music.

From across the fields you sometimes can hear a nervous dog barking and somebody else's dog answering from across the creek. You even like to listen to the corn blades whispering to each other as the wind blows through them.

Summer nights on our farm even *smell* good. Nearly always there is the smell of new-mown hay or pine tree fragrance, which is always sweeter at night. If you are near the creek, you can smell the fish that don't want to bite, and the wild peppermint, the sweet clover, and a thousand other half-friendly, half-lonely smells that make you feel sad and glad at the same time.

Things you *think* at night are wonderful, too. You can lie on the grass in the yard in the summertime and look up at the purplish blue sky—which is like a big upside-down sieve with a million white holes in it—and in your mind go sailing out across the Milky Way like a boy skating on the bayou pond, dodging this way and that so you won't run into any of the stars.

But this wasn't the right time to hear or see or smell how wonderful a night it was. It was, instead, a time for two worried boys, including a red-haired, freckle-faced one, to get inside the tent and into bed and to sleep.

Pretty soon Poetry and I were at the rail fence across from our mailbox. There we stopped, keeping ourselves in the shadow of the elderberry bush that grew there. It seemed the moonlight had never been brighter, and we couldn't afford to let ourselves be seen or heard by anybody.

I was shivering with the cold, and just that second I sneezed.

Poetry shushed me with a shush that was almost louder than my sneeze, and he whispered, "Hey, don't wake anybody up! Your father has told us for the last time to—"

"Shush, yourself!" I ordered him.

We decided to go along the fence and cross the road by the hickory nut trees, then climb over into our cornfield and sneak down between the corn rows to arrive at the tent from the opposite side. That way, nobody could see us from the house. So we did.

We had to pass Old Red Addie's apartment hog house on the way, which is the kind of place on a farm that *doesn't* have a nice, clean, sweet farm smell. Pretty soon, though, still shivering and wishing I had dry nightclothes to sleep in, we were behind the tent, waiting and listening to see if we could get in without being seen or heard.

Right then I sneezed again, and I knew I was either going to catch a cold or I already had one. I quickly lifted the tent flap and swished through the plastic screen, expecting Poetry to follow me.

But he didn't and wouldn't. He stood for a second in the clear moonlight that came slanting through a branchless place in the plum tree overhead. Then he said, "I'll be back in a minute." And he started toward the house—*in the moonlight, where he could be seen!*

"Wait!" I called to him in as quiet a whisper as I could. "Where are you going?"

"I'm *thirsty*," he whispered back. "I forgot to get a drink at the spring."

"You'll wake up my *father!*" I exclaimed. "Don't you *dare* pump that pump handle!"

But Poetry couldn't be stopped, and I knew that if Dad ever waked up and came out to prove he had meant what he had said, there'd *really* be trouble. He would hear me sneeze or see my wet nightclothes, and he would wonder what on earth and why.

So in a second, like the old story in one of our schoolbooks about a man named Mr. McGregor chasing Peter Rabbit, who was all wet from having jumped into a can of water to hide—and Peter Rabbit sneezing—in a second I was acting out that story backward. I myself was a very wet, very dumb bunny chasing Leslie Poetry Thompson to try to stop him from getting us into even more trouble than we were already in.

We arrived at the pitcher pump platform at the same time, where I hissed to him not to pump the pump. I pushed in between him and the pump, blocking him from doing what his stubborn mind was driving him to do.

"I'm *thirsty,*" he squawked.

"The pump handle squeaks!" I hissed back to him and shoved him off the platform. My wet left pajama sleeve pressed against his face.

What happened after that happened so fast and with so much noise it would have wakened seventeen fathers. Poetry, my almost best friend, who had always stood by me when I was in trouble, who was always on my side, all of a sudden didn't act as if he was my friend at all.

We weren't any more than three feet from the large iron kettle filled with innocent water, which up to that moment had been reflecting the moon as clearly as if it had been a mirror—

clearly enough, in fact, for you to see the man in the moon in it.

The next second, Poetry's powerful arms were around me, and he was dragging me and himself toward that big kettle. The next second after that, he scooped my eighty-nine pounds up and, with me kicking and squirming and trying to wriggle out of his grasp and not being able to, he set me down *kerplop-splash, double-splashety-slump* right in the center of that large kettle of water.

"What on *earth!*" I cried, my voice trembling with temper, my teeth chattering with the cold, and my mind whirling.

My words exploded out of my mouth at the very minute Dad exploded out the back door. "'What on earth' is right," he exclaimed in his big father-sounding voice. "What on earth are you doing in the *water?*"

Poetry answered for me, saying politely, "It's all my fault, Mr. Collins. We were getting a drink and I—I shouldn't have done it, but I pushed him in. I—" Then Poetry's voice took on a mischievous tone as he said, "The water was so clear and the man in the moon reflected in it was so handsome, I wanted to see what a good-looking *boy* would look like in it. I couldn't resist the temptation."

Such an innocent voice! *So* polite! I was boiling inside as I splashed myself out of the kettle and stood dripping on the pump platform.

Then I did get a surprise. Dad's voice, instead of being like black thunder, which it sometimes is at a time like that, was a sort of husky whisper. "Let's keep quiet—all of us. We wouldn't want to wake up your mother, Bill. You boys get back into the tent quick, while I slip into the house and get Bill a pair of dry pajamas. Hurry up! *Quick,* into the tent!"

He turned, tiptoed to the back screen door, and opened it quietly while Poetry and I scooted to the tent. A second later we were inside, standing in the shadowy moonlight that oozed in through the plastic window above my cot.

Dad was back out of the house almost before I was out of my wet pajamas. He whispered to us at the tent door, "Here's a towel. Dry yourself good. Put these fresh pajamas on —but *be quiet!*" He whispered the last two words almost savagely. "Here, let me have your old wet ones. I'll hang them on the line behind the house to dry. And remember, not a word of this to your mother, Bill. Do you hear me?"

"Don't worry," I said. It was easy to hear anything as easy to listen to as that.

Then Dad was gone.

In only a few jiffies I was dry and had on my nice, fresh, clean-smelling, stripeless yellow pajamas, and there wasn't even a sniffle in my nose to hint that maybe I would catch cold.

Boy oh boy, was it ever quiet in the tent! The only sounds were those in my mind. Everything had happened so fast that it seemed as if it all had taken only a minute. But it also seemed as though a year had passed. So many exciting things had happened—crazy things, too, such as a boy galloping around on a green watermelon in a pool of cold water while a gang of girls screamed like wild hyenas that there was a zebra taking a bath in the spring.

"Wait," Poetry ordered, as I sat down on the edge of my cot and started to crawl in. "We can't get in between your mother's nice clean sheets with feet that have waded through mud and dusty cornfields. I'll go get the wash pan from the grape arbor, fill it with water, and bring it back."

"You stay *here!*" I ordered. "I don't trust you out of this tent one minute! I'll get the water myself."

And do you know what that dumb bunny answered me? He said in his very polite voice, "But I'm thirsty. I haven't had a chance to get a drink. I—"

"Stay *here!*" I ordered again. "I'll *bring* you a drink."

"After all I've done for you, you won't even let me go with you?" he begged.

"What have you done for me, I'd like to know? You—with your plunking me into the middle of that kettle of water!"

Poetry grabbed me by the shoulders and shook me. "Listen, pal," he said fiercely, "I saved you out of big trouble. I heard your father opening the back door, and I knew he'd be there in a minute. If he found you all wet with that *spring*water, he'd have asked you how come, and you'd really have been in a pretty kettle. So I pushed you in. Don't you see?"

Well, I decided maybe Poetry really had been my friend. Besides, if I let him go to get a pan of water for washing our feet, and if Dad did see and hear him, Dad would probably not say a word—not wanting to wake Mom up.

"All right," I said with a sigh, "but hurry back."

Which he did.

Pretty soon we had our feet washed and dried on the towel. When we got through, I noticed that the towel might also have to be washed in the morning.

In only a little while we were in our cots again and, I guess, sound asleep, for right away I began dreaming a crazy mixed-up dream. I was running in red-striped pajamas through the woods, leaving the path made by boys' bare feet and working my way along the crest of the hill where the papaw bushes were, just to see how many girl campers there were. Then it seemed I was in the spring again, galloping around on a green no-legged bronco, which somebody had stolen and plugged and maybe sold to the girls. Or maybe some of the girls had invaded our melon patch that very night and stolen it themselves.

I hated to think that, though, because any girl who is a Girl Scout is supposed to be like a boy who is a Boy Scout, which is absolutely honest. Besides, as much as I didn't like girls—not most of them, anyway—and was scared of them a little, it seemed there was a small voice inside of me that all my life had been whispering that girls are kind of special. Anybody couldn't help it if she happened to be born one. Mom had been a girl for quite a few years herself, and it hadn't hurt her a bit. She had grown up to become one of the most wonderful people in the world.

But who had stolen my watermelon? And how had *it* gotten down there in the spring? It *was* my melon, of course!

The idea woke me up. Or else my own voice did when I heard myself saying to Poetry, "Hey, you! *Poetry!* Come on, wake up!"

He groaned, turned over in his cot, and groaned again. "Let me sleep, will you?"

"No," I whispered, "wake up! Come on and go with me. I've got to go down into our watermelon patch to see—"

"I don't want any more water," he mumbled, "and I wouldn't think you would either."

"That melon in the spring," I said. "I just dreamed it was my prize melon! I think somebody stole it. I want to go down to our garden to see if it's gone."

Then Poetry showed that he hadn't been asleep at all. He rolled over, sat up, swung his feet out over the edge of his cot and onto the canvas floor, and I knew we were *both* going outside once more—*just once more.*

What we were going to do was one of the most important things we had ever done, even if it might not seem so to a boy's father if he should happen to wake up and see us in the melon patch and think we were two strange boys out there stealing watermelons.

Pretty soon Poetry and I were outside the tent again in the wonderful moonlight, where now most of the cicadas had stopped their whirring and the crickets had begun to take over for the rest of the night. Fireflies were everywhere, too. It seemed there were thousands of them flashing their green lights on and off in every tree in our orchard and in all the open spaces everywhere. The lights of those that were flying were like short, yellowish green chalk marks being made on a schoolhouse blackboard.

Poetry, with his flashlight, was leading the way as he and I moved out across our barnyard. At the wooden gate near the barn, he said, "Hear that, will you?"

I listened, but all I could hear was the sound of pigeons cooing in the haymow. The low, lonesome cooing of pigeons is one of the friendliest sounds a boy ever hears.

There are certainly a lot of different sounds around our farm. I have learned to imitate nearly all of them so well that I sound like a farmyard full of animals sometimes, Dad says. Mom also says that sometimes I actually *look* like a red-haired, freckle-faced pig—which I probably don't.

Did you ever stop to think about all the different kinds of sounds a country boy gets to enjoy?

While you are imagining Poetry and me cutting across the south pasture to the east side of our melon patch, I'll mention just a few that we get to hear a hundred times a year: the wind roaring in a winter blizzard, Dragonfly's dad's bulls bellowing, Circus's dad's hounds baying or bawling or snarling or growling, our black-and-white cat meowing or purring, mice squeaking in the corncrib, Old Topsy neighing, Poetry's dad's sheep bleating, all the old setting hens clucking, the laying hens singing or cackling, Big Jim's folks' ducks quacking, honeybees and bumblebees droning and buzzing, crows cawing, our red rooster crowing at midnight or just at daybreak, screech owls screeching, hoot owls hooting, cicadas drumming, crickets chirping. And Dragonfly sneezing, especially in ragweed season, which it already was in the Sugar Creek territory.

There are also a lot of interesting sounds down along the creek and the bayou too, such as water singing in the riffles, the big night herons going *"Quoke-quoke,"* cardinals whistling, bobwhites calling, squirrels barking. And when the gang is together, the happiest sounds of all are with everybody talking at once and nobody listening to anybody.

There are also a few sounds that hurt your ears, such as Dad filing a saw, Old Red Addie's family of piglets squealing, the death squawk of a chicken just before it gets its head chopped off for the Collins family's dinner, and the wild screeches of a bevy of girls calling an innocent boy in red-striped pajamas a *zebra!*

In only a few minutes we were out in the middle of our garden, looking to see if any melons were missing. I was just sure that when I came to Ida's vine, I'd find a long oval indentation where she had been. The dream I had had about her being stolen was so real in my mind.

"All this walk for nothing," Poetry exclaimed all of a sudden, when his flashlight beam landed *ker-flash* right on the fat green side of Ida Watermelon Collins, as peaceful and quiet as an old setting hen on her nest.

I stood looking down at her proudly, then I said in a grumpy voice, "What do you mean, making me get up out of a comfortable bed and drag myself all the way out here for nothing! You see to it that you don't make me dream such a crazy dream again. Do you hear me?"

I felt better after saying that.

Then Poetry grunted grouchily and said, "And don't ever rob *me* of my good night's rest again, either!"

With that, we started to wend our way back across the melon field in the direction of the barn again.

We hadn't gone more than a few yards when what to my wondering ears should come but the strange sound of something running. That is, that's what it sounded like at first. I stopped and looked around in a fast moonlit circle of directions. Then I saw, away over by the new woven wire fence near the iron pitcher pump, something dark and about the size of a long, low-bodied extralarge raccoon, moving toward the shadows of the elderberry bushes.

I could feel the red hair on the back of my neck and on the top of my head beginning to crawl like the bristles on a dog's or a cat's or a hog's back do when it's angry, except that I wasn't angry—not yet, anyway.

A little later, though, I was not only angry, but my mind was going in excited circles. If you had been me and seen what I saw and found out what I found out, you'd have felt the way I felt. I was all mixed up in my thoughts, worried and excited and stormy-minded, and ready for a headfirst dive into the middle of one of the most thrilling mysteries that ever started in the middle of a dog day's night.

3

Y ou don't have to wait long to decide what to
do at a time like that—not when you have
mischievous-minded, quick-thinking Poetry along
with you, even if you are in the middle of a
muddle in the middle of a melon patch, watching something the size of a long, very fat raccoon hurrying in jerky movements toward the
shadows of the elderberry bushes.

If things hadn't been so exciting, it would
have been a good time to let my imagination
put on wings and fly me around in my boy's
world awhile. A million stars were all over the
sky, and fireflies were writing on the blackboard of the night and rubbing out all their
greenish yellow marks as fast as they made
them. And the crickets were singing, and the
smell of sweet clover was enough to make you
dizzy with just feeling fine.

But it was no time for dreaming. Instead, it
was a time for acting—and *quick!*

"Come on!" Poetry whispered. "Let's chase
him!" and he started running and yelling,
"Stop, thief! Stop!"

Away we both went, out across the garden,
dodging melons as we went, leaping over them
or swerving aside as we do when we are on a
coon chase at night with Circus's dad's long-

eared, long-nosed, long-voiced hounds leading the way. We were trying to catch up with that dark brown, long, low, very fat animal—something I had never seen around Sugar Creek before in all my life.

Then, all of a disappointing sudden, the brown whatever-it-was disappeared into the shadow of the elderberry bushes, and I heard a whirring noise in the lane on the other side of the fence. Then something came to noisy-motored life, a pair of headlights went on, and an old-sounding car went rattling down the lane, headed in the direction of the Sugar Creek School, which is at the end of the lane, where it meets the county line road.

Poetry's big flashlight shot a straight white beam through the night. It landed *ker-flash* right on that old-looking car as it rattled past the iron pitcher pump and disappeared down the hill. A few seconds later, we heard it go *rat-tlety-crash* across the board floor of the branch bridge. The headlights lit up the lane as it sped up the hill on the other side in the direction of the schoolhouse.

What on earth!

My mind was still on the car and who might be in it when I heard Poetry say, "Look there! There's our wild animal! He stopped right at the fence! Let's get him!"

My mind came back to the long, brown, low, very fat something-or-other we had been chasing a minute before. My eyes got to it at about the same time Poetry's flashlight beam socked it *ker-wham-flash* right in the middle of its fat side.

"What is it?" I exclaimed, looking about for a stick or a club to protect myself in case I had to.

My imagination had been yelling to me, *It's some kind of animal, different from anything you've ever seen!* So I was terribly disappointed when Poetry let out a disgusted grunt of surprise, saying, "Aw, it's only an old gunnysack."

And it was. A light brown gunnysack with something large inside of it. Fastened to one end was a plastic rope that stretched from the gunnysack back into the elderberry bushes.

Whatever was in the sack wasn't moving, not even breathing, I thought, as we stood studying it and wondering, *What on earth?*

It was large and long and round and very fat and—

Then, like a light turning on in my mind, I knew what was in that brown burlap bag. I knew it as well as I knew my name was Bill Collins, Theodore Collins's only son. "There's a watermelon in that bag!" I exclaimed.

Whoever was in that car must have crawled out into our garden, picked the melon, slipped it into this gunnysack, tied the rope to it, and had been hiding here in the bushes while pulling the rope and dragging the melon to him! Doing it that way so that nobody would see him carrying it off!

Was I ever stirred up in my mind! Yet, there wasn't any sense in getting too stirred up. A boy couldn't let himself waste his perfectly good temper in one big explosion, because, as my dad has told me many a time, you can't think straight when you're angry. Dad was trying to teach me to *use* my temper instead of *losing* it.

"A temper is a fine thing if you control it but not if it controls you," he has told me maybe five hundred times in my half-long life. My hot temper had gotten me into trouble many a time by shoving me headfirst into an unnecessary fight with somebody who didn't know how to control his own temper.

In a flash I was down on my haunches beside the gunnysack. "Here," I said to Poetry, "lend me your knife a minute. Let's get this old burlap bag off and see if it's a watermelon!"

"Goose!" Poetry answered me. "I'm wearing my pajamas!"

Both of us were, of course. In fact, we both looked ridiculous there in the moonlight.

"See!" Poetry exclaimed. "Here's how they were going to get it through the fence!"

My eyes fastened onto the circle of light his flashlight made on a spot back under the elderberry bushes. Then I noticed there was a hole cut in Dad's new woven wire fence, large enough to let a boy through. Boy oh boy, would Dad ever have a hard time using *his* temper when he saw that tomorrow morning!

But we had to do something with the melon. "Let's leave it for the gang to see tomorrow," Poetry suggested. "Let Big Jim decide what to do about it."

"What to do about Bob Till, you mean," I said grimly. Already my temper was telling me it was Bob Till himself, the Sugar Creek Gang's worst enemy, who had been trying to steal one of our melons.

Just thinking that started my blood to running faster in my veins. How many times during the past two years we had had trouble with John Till's oldest boy, Bob! And how many times Big Jim, the Sugar Creek Gang's fierce-fighting leader, had had to give Bob a licking! And always Bob was just as bad a boy afterward and maybe even worse.

I was remembering that only last week at our very latest gang meeting by the spring, Big Jim had told us, "I'm *through* fighting Bob Till. I'm going to try kindness. We're *all* going to try it. Let's show him that a Christian boy doesn't have to fight every time somebody knocks a chip off his shoulder. And let's not put a chip on our shoulder in the first place."

At that meeting, Dragonfly had piped up and asked, "What's a 'chip on your shoulder' mean?"

Poetry had answered for Big Jim, saying, "It's a doubled-up fist shaking itself under somebody else's nose and daring him to hit you first!"

Big Jim ignored Poetry's supposed-to-be-funny answer and said, "Bob's on probation, you know, and he has to behave, or the sentence that is hanging over him will go into effect and he'll have to spend a year in reform school. We wouldn't want that. We have got to help him prove that he can behave himself. If he thinks we're mad at him, he'll be tempted to do things to get even with us. As long as this sentence is hang—"

Dragonfly cut in then with one of his not so bright questions, at the same time trying to show how smart he was in school. "What kind of a sentence—*declarative* or *interrogative* or *imperative* or *exclamatory?*"

Big Jim's jaw set, and he gave Dragonfly an exclamatory look. Then he went on talking, shocking us almost out of our wits when he told us something not a one of us knew yet. "One of the conditions of his being on probation instead of in reform school is that he go to church at least once a week for a year. That means he'll probably come to *our* church, and *that* means he'll be in our Sunday school class, and—"

Well, I got one of the strangest feelings I ever had in my life. Whirlwindlike thoughts were spiraling in my mind. I just couldn't imagine Bob Till in church and Sunday school in the first place. It would certainly seem funny to have him there with nice clothes on and his hair combed, listening to our preacher preach from the Bible. What if I had to sit beside him myself—I, who could hardly think his name without feeling my muscles tighten and my fists start to double up?

Another thing Big Jim told us at that meeting was: "You guys want to promise that you will stick with me and all of us try to help him?"

We had promised.

And now here was Bob already doing something that would make the sentence drop on his head. Whoever was in that car just *had* to be Bob Till, because he had a car just like that—it sounding like a real hot rod.

"Listen!" Poetry exclaimed. I listened in every direction there was. Then I heard and saw at the same time a car coming back up the lane. Its headlights were going to hit us full in the face.

"Quick!" Poetry cried. "Down!"

We stooped low behind the elderberry bushes and waited for the car to pass.

"It's slowing down. It's going to stop," I said.

Which it did. The same rattling old jalopy.

In a split second we were scooting along the fencerow to a spot several feet farther up the lane. And there we crouched behind some giant ragweeds and goldenrod and black-eyed Susans. Dad had told me a week ago to cut down the ragweeds with our scythe, and I hadn't done it yet. I nearly always cut the goldenrod too, because Dragonfly, the pop-eyed member of our gang, is allergic to them as well as to ragweed, and he nearly always uses this lane going to and from school.

My heart was pounding in my ears as I crouched there with Poetry, he in his green-striped pajamas and I in my plain yellow ones.

"Get down!" I told him.

"I am down," he whispered.

"Flatter!" I ordered. "So you won't be seen! Can't you lie *flat*?"

"I can only lie round," he answered. That, under any other circumstances, would have sounded funny, since he was so extralarge around.

"Somebody is getting out," Poetry whispered.

"How many are there?"

"Only one, I think."

Then I felt Poetry's body grow tense. "There goes one of your watermelons," he whispered.

I saw it at the same time he did. The brown burlap bag was being pulled deeper into the elderberry bushes, and I knew somebody was stealing one of our melons. In a minute it would be gone!

"Let's jump him," I exclaimed to Poetry. My blood was tingling for battle. I started to my feet.

But he stopped me, saying, *"Sh!"* in a subdued but savage whisper. "Detectives don't stop a man from stealing. They let him do it first, then they capture him."

It wasn't easy to do nothing, watching that watermelon being hoisted into the backseat of that car. My muscles were aching to get into some new kind of action that was different from hoeing potatoes, milking cows, gathering eggs, and other things any ordinary boy's muscles could do. I was straining to go tearing up the fencerow to the elderberry bushes, dive through the hole in the fence, make a football-style tackle on that thief's legs, and bring him down. If all the gang were there, I was pretty sure one or the other of us would not be able to stay crouching stock-still. He would rush in, and the rest of us would be like Jack in the poem about "Jack and Jill"—we would go tumbling after, even if some of us got knocked down and got our crowns cracked.

But the rest of the gang wasn't there. Besides, it was already too late to do anything. In less time than it has taken me to write it, the melon in the gunnysack was in the car, the thief was in the driver's seat, and the hot rod was shooting like an arrow with two blazing headlights down the moonlit lane.

Poetry shot his powerful flashlight beam straight after the car, socking it on the license plate. And I knew that his mind—which is so good it's almost like what is called a "photographic mind"—would remember the number *if* he had been able to see it.

Well, it's like having a big blown-up balloon suddenly burst in your face to have your exciting adventure come to an end like that. It's also kind of how a fish must feel when it's nibbling on a fat fishing worm down in Sugar Creek and, all of a disappointing sudden, has its nice juicy dinner jerked away from it by the fisherman who is on the other end of the line.

There wasn't anything left to do except go back to the tent and to bed and to sleep.

Just thinking that reminded me of the fact

that I probably would need *another* pair of pajamas to sleep in. The yellow pair I had on had gotten soiled while I was lying in the grass behind the goldenrod and ragweed and black-eyed Susans. "We'll have to wash our feet again before we can crawl into Mom's nice clean sheets," I said as we started back to the tent.

"Maybe it would be easier and cause less worry for your mother if we just climbed into our cots and went to sleep. Tomorrow, if your mother gets angry at us, we can explain about the watermelon, and that will get her angry at the thief instead of at us. We could offer to help her wash the sheets, anyway."

It was a pair of very sad, very mad boys that threaded their way through the watermelon patch to the pasture and across it to the gate at the barn and on toward the tent.

There were still a few cicadas busy with their drums, I noticed, in spite of the fact that I was all stirred up in my mind about the watermelon.

Thinking about the seeds in their long, straight rows, buried in the dark red flesh of the watermelon the way seeds always are, just as if somebody had planted them, reminded me of the stars in the sky overhead. I was wishing I could look up and see the Dog Star, which is the brightest star in all the Sugar Creek sky. But during "dog days," which are the hot and sultry days of July and August, you have to get up in the *morning* to see it, because the Dog Star comes up with the sun in July and August. Then, in a very little while, it fades out of sight.

In February, the Dog Star is almost straight overhead at night and is like a shining star at the top of a Christmas tree. But who wants to go out in the middle of a zero-cold night just to look at a star, even if it is the brightest one that ever shines?

"Are you sleepy?" Poetry asked when we reached the plum tree.

"Not very," I said. "But I'm still so mad I can't see straight."

"You want to go back down to the spring with me?" he asked, his hand on the tent flap, about to lift it for us to go in.

"Are you crazy?" I asked.

"I'm a detective. I want to go down there and see if we can find the waxed paper you threw away when we heard those girls at the top of the hill."

"My mother has dozens of old bread wrappers," I told him. "I'll ask her for one for you in the morning."

"Listen, pal," Poetry whispered as he let the tent flap drop into place and grabbed me by the arm. "I said I'm a detective, and I'm looking for a clue! I've a hunch there was something *in* that paper— something whoever put it in that melon didn't want to get wet!"

Well, I knew, from having studied about watermelons that summer, that the edible part of a watermelon is made up of such things as protein, and fat, and ash, and calcium, and sugar, and water, and just fiber. Six percent of the melon is sugar and more than 92 percent is water. You could eat a piece of watermelon the size of Charlotte Ann's head, and it would be like drinking more than a pint of sweetened water. I could understand that anything anybody put on the inside of a watermelon would get wet, almost as wet as if you had dunked it in a pail of water.

"Look," I said to Poetry, "I don't want to show my face or risk my neck anywhere near a campful of excitable girls who can't tell a boy in a pair of red-striped pajamas from a zebra. They might start screaming bloody murder if they happened to see us again."

"I'll have to go alone, then," Poetry announced firmly. And in seconds, his green-striped back was all I could see of him as he waddled off across the moonlit lawn toward the walnut tree and the gate.

It was either let him go alone on a wild-goose chase or go with him and run the risk of stumbling into a whirlwind of honest-to-goodness trouble.

I caught up to him by the time he had reached our mailbox. I whispered, "What do you think might have been wrapped up in it?"

Poetry's voice sounded mysterious and also very serious as he answered, "Didn't you read the paper this morning?"

I nearly always read the daily paper—part of it, anyway—almost as soon as it landed in the mailbox. Sometimes I'd race to get to the box before Dad did. Dad himself always read the editorials. Mom read the fashions and the new recipes and the accidents. She also *worried* about the accidents out loud to Dad a little. Mom always felt especially sad whenever anything happened to a little baby.

"Sure," I puffed to Poetry as I loped along after him in the shadowy moonlight. "What's that got to do with a wad of waxed paper in a plugged watermelon?"

His answer, panted back over his shoulder, started the shivers vibrating in my spine again. If I had been a cicada with a sound-producing organ inside me somewhere, my shaking thoughts would have filled the whole woods with noise.

Poetry's gasping words were: "Whoever broke into the supermarket last week might be hiding out in this part of the county—maybe even along the creek here somewhere!"

"The paper didn't say that," I said.

"It didn't have to," Poetry shouted back. "It didn't say *where* he was hiding, did it? I've got a hunch he's right here in our territory. Maybe in the swamp or—"

I'd had a lot of experiences with Poetry's hunches, and he'd been right so many times that, whenever he said he had one, I felt myself suddenly getting in a mood for a big surprise of some kind.

But this time his idea didn't quite seem to make sense. So I said, "Who on earth would want to stuff a lot of money inside a *watermelon*?"

Poetry's answer was a grouchy grunt, followed by a scolding. "I said I had a *hunch!* I *know* we'll find something important going on around here. Now, stop asking dumb questions and hurry up!" With that, the detective-minded boy set a still faster pace for me as we dashed down the hill to the place where I had just had the humiliating experience of riding a wild, green, legless bronco in a reservoir full of cold water.

The red-striped pajamas I had been wearing must have made me look ridiculous to those Girl Scouts, I thought. I hoped they wouldn't come back to the spring again while Poetry and I were looking for what he called a "clue."

4

Several times before that night was finally over, I thought how much more sensible we would have been if we had curled ourselves up on our cots in the tent and gone sound asleep.

It's better to be in bed when you have your pajamas on than scouting a watermelon patch, or splashing in a pool of springwater, or crouching shivering behind ragweeds and goldenrod and black-eyed Susans in a fencerow, or searching with a flashlight for a wad of waxed paper that somebody had stuffed into a watermelon.

Especially is it better to be in bed, as any decent boy should be, than to be lying on your stomach under an evergreen with pine needles pricking you, while you don't dare move or you'll be heard by somebody you are straining your eyes to see, and while your friend does the most ridiculous thing you ever heard of at the very spring where you yourself were just an hour ago.

Boy oh boy, let me tell you about what happened the second time Poetry and I went to the spring.

When we came to the beech tree, on whose close-grained gray bark the gang and maybe thirty other people had carved their initials through the years, we stopped to look the situation over. There was a stretch of moonlit open space between us and the leaning linden tree, which is at the top of the slope leading down to the spring.

The shadowy hulk of the old Black Widow Stump in the middle of the moonlit space looked like a black ghost. I kept straining my ears in the direction of the linden tree, wondering if there might be anybody down at the spring. Then I focused my ears and my eyes in the direction of the papaw bushes, away off to the left, where the girls' camp was. I could smell the odor of wet ashes, and I knew that the girls had had a campfire near the Black Widow Stump. There was an outdoor fireplace there for picnickers to use for wiener roasts, steak fries, making coffee, and for just giving a picnic a friendly atmosphere. I was only half glad to notice that the girls had put out the very last spark of their fire, because I hated to have to admit that a flock of girls knew one of the most important safety rules of a good camper, which is: "Never leave a campfire burning, but put it out before you go."

From the beech tree we moved east a little way, then made a moonlit dash for the row of evergreens that border the rail fence skirting the top of the hill above the bayou.

"OK," Poetry panted when we got there. "We'll work our way down from here. As soon as we get to the bottom, we'll turn on the light and start looking for our clue."

And then I heard something. It was a noise

out in the creek somewhere. It was the sound of an oar in a rowlock.

Poetry and I hushed each other at the same time and strained our ears in the direction the sound had come from. At the same instant, we dropped down onto the pine needles under the tree.

"It's somebody in a boat," Poetry whispered. "He's pulling in at the spring."

I could see the boat now, emerging from the shadow of the trees down the shore. It had come up the creek from the direction of the Sugar Creek bridge.

Now the boat was being steered toward the shore. I knew if it was anybody who knew the shoreline, he wouldn't stop directly in front of the spring, because the overflow drained into the creek there and it would be a muddy landing. Below it, or just above it, was a good place.

"There's only one man in it," Poetry said. Even in the shadowy moonlight I could tell that it was a red boat and one we'd never seen before.

Then I did get a surprise, and my whole mind began whirling with wondering what on earth in a gunnysack! No sooner had the prow of the boat touched the gravelly shore than whoever was in it was up and out and beaching the boat, wrapping the guy rope, which is called a "painter," around the small maple that grew there. Then he stepped back into the boat, stooped, and picked up something in both hands—something dark and long and . . .

Hey! my mind's voice was screaming, while my actual voice was keeping still. *It's a gunny-sack! It's the brown burlap bag we saw in the watermelon patch a half hour ago!*

In a minute the man was out of the boat again and disappearing up the path in the shadow of the trees. A second later he emerged at the opening in the board fence, worked his way through, and moved straight toward the spring, lugging the burlap bag with the melon in it.

"Let's jump him!" I whispered to Poetry.

Poetry put his lips to my ear and whispered back, "Nothing doing. Detectives don't capture a criminal *before* he commits a crime. They let him do it first, *then* they capture him!"

"He's already done it," I said, "at the melon patch!"

"If you'll be patient," Poetry whispered back, "we'll find out what we want to know."

We kept on watching from behind the evergreen while the man at the spring hoisted his burlap bag over the cement edge of the pool and let it down inside. He stayed in a stooping, stock-still position for several seconds, then began doing something with his hands.

"He's about the size of Big Jim," I whispered to Poetry.

"Or Circus," he answered.

"Big Jim," I insisted, but I knew that neither of *them* would steal a watermelon and bring it here by night in a boat.

Just then I shifted my position a little

because I had been sitting on my foot and it was beginning to hurt. It was a crazy time to lose my balance and have to struggle awkwardly to keep from sliding down the incline, but that is what I did. And for a few anxious seconds I was looking after myself instead of watching the mysterious movements at the spring.

By the time I was focusing my vision in his direction again, the man or extralarge boy—whichever he was—had left the spring and was on his way back to the boat. For a minute we lost sight of him in the shadows. Then we saw him again. He was standing at the boat with his back to us, and we heard the painter being unwrapped from the tree.

In only a few more seconds the boat was gliding out into the creek. It went only a few feet, though, and almost right away the oarsman steered it toward the shore, where it became only a dim outline among the shadow of the trees that grew along the steep slope.

Poetry sighed an exasperated sigh and said, "Well, it wasn't any of *our* gang, anyway. See?"

I had already seen—first the flash of a match or a cigarette lighter, then a reddish glow in the dark, and I knew somebody was smoking. That's how we knew for sure it wasn't any of the gang.

"I'd like to get my hands on him for just one minute," I said to Poetry. "Both hands—twenty times—in fast succession."

"You wouldn't strike a woman or a girl, would you?" he answered.

"What? Who said it was a woman or a girl? He had on a pair of pants, didn't he?"

"Girls wear slacks, don't they? And lots of girls smoke, too."

"And shouldn't," I answered.

We crept from our hiding place, scrambled down to where the boat had been beached, and looked to be sure the oarsman—or oarswoman—was out of sight. Then we slipped through the fence to look for the melon in the cement pool and also to look around for the wad of paper I had tossed away when we had been there before.

It was an interesting two or three minutes, because that's all the time it took us to discover something important—very, very important!

Did you ever have a flashlight beam strike you full in the face and blind you for a few seconds? Well, the white light from that match or cigarette lighter and the reddish glow from the cigarette or cigar fifty yards down the shore sort of blinded me—not my eyes, but my mind. I couldn't think straight for a minute. It was Poetry's suggestion, though—that the thief might be a woman or a girl—that really confused me.

I guess all the time I had had in the back of my mind that the thief was Bob Till. But what if the person in the boat *was* a girl? No wonder I couldn't think.

It was the perfume that sent my mind whirling. We'd noticed it the very second we crawled through the fence. It was so strong it made the whole place smell as if somebody had upset the perfume counter in the Sugar Creek Dime Store, and half the bottles of cologne and fancy perfumes had been broken.

If Dragonfly had been with us, I thought, he'd have sneezed and sneezed and sneezed because he's allergic to almost every perfume there is.

Well, here was our chance to make a quick search for the wad of waxed paper, which is what we had come there for in the first place. I remembered just about where I had tossed it, and in only a few seconds Poetry whispered, "Here it is! Here's our clue!"

His excitement about the thing, and his being so sure, had built up my mind to expect to see something wonderful inside that waxed paper. Anybody who would go to the trouble to steal a watermelon and deliver it secretly in a boat at night would probably leave something *in* the melon worth a hundred times more than the melon itself.

There in the shadow of the linden tree, to the music of the bubbling water in the spring and the singing of the crickets, Poetry held the flashlight while my trembling fingers unfolded that crumpled piece of waxed paper and spread it out.

"There's *printing* on it!" Poetry exclaimed under his breath.

"What does it say?" I asked.

"It says—it says, *'Eat more Eatmore Bread. It's*

better for you. The more Eatmore you eat, the more you like it.'"

It was disgusting. Very disappointing also.

"Smell it," Poetry said.

I did, and boy oh boy—there was *really* a perfume odor around the place now! If Dragonfly had been there, I thought again—or rather, I started to think. I didn't get to finish.

All of a sudden from the crest of the hill I heard a rustling of last year's dry leaves. Then I saw a flashlight leading the way and a spindle-legged barefoot boy in red-striped pajamas coming down the hill to the spring. Imagine *that!* Dragonfly in his nightclothes! What on earth!

Poetry and I slipped behind an undergrowth of small elms, where we couldn't be seen, and listened and watched as Dragonfly came all the way down. He went straight to the cement pool and shone his flashlight inside. Then his hands began to work fast as if he was in a big hurry and also as if he was scared and wanted to do what he was doing and get it over quick. He certainly was nervous, and he seemed to be having trouble getting done what he wanted to do.

Poetry's face was close to mine. I decided I could whisper into his ear and only he would hear me, so I said, "Look! He's got a knife! He's going to plug the melon! He—"

Poetry jammed his elbow into my ribs so hard that it made me grunt out loud.

Dragonfly jumped as though he was shot,

dropped his knife into the spring, started to straighten up, lost his balance, staggered in several directions, then went *ker-whammety-swish-splash* into the water just as I myself had done an hour or so before.

And there he was, as I had been—a very wet boy in some very wet, very cold water, struggling to get onto his feet and out of the pool and sneezing and spluttering because he had probably gotten water into his mouth or nose and maybe even into his lungs.

And now what should we do?

We didn't have time to decide. Right that second there was the sound of running steps at the top of the incline. Two shadowy figures with flashlights came flying down that leaf-strewn path, and somebody's voice that was as plain as day a girl's voice cried, "We've got you, you little rascal!"

Those two girls swooped down upon Dragonfly, seized him by the collar, and started dunking him in the pool, dunking and splashing water over him and saying, "Take that—and that—and *that!* We knew if we waited here, you'd be back!"

Then, all of a sudden, there was a hullabaloo of other girls' voices at the top of the incline, and a shower of flashlights and excited words came tumbling down with them. It seemed there must have been a dozen girls, though there probably weren't. Like a herd of stampeding calves, all of them swarmed around our little half-scared-to-death Dragonfly, who was shivering and probably wondering what on earth. They were pulling him this way and that, as if they would tear him to pieces.

Things such as what I was seeing and hearing that minute just don't happen. Yet they *were* happening and to one of the grandest little guys who ever sneezed in hay fever season—our very own Dragonfly himself.

I didn't know what he had done or why, but it seemed that anybody with *that* many people swarming all over him like a colony of angry bumblebees ought to have somebody to stand up for him. If it had been a gang of boys beating up on that innocent little guy, I probably would have made a football-style dive into the thick of them and bowled half a dozen of them over into the cement pool. Then I'd have turned loose my two doubled-up, experienced fists on them, windmill fashion, and Poetry would have come tumbling after.

But what do you do when your pal is being torn to pieces by a pack of helpless girls? As I have maybe told you before, my parents had taught me to respect all girls, sort of as though they were angels, which most of them aren't. The only one I ever saw in the whole Sugar Creek territory who is anywhere near to being an angel is one of Circus's many sisters, whose name is Lucille. Also, I wouldn't have the heart to fight a weak-muscled helpless creature that men and boys are supposed to defend from all harm and danger.

Right that minute, though, while they were

dunking Dragonfly in the spring and shoving him around and calling him names, it didn't seem girls *were* such helpless creatures. Certainly it was Dragonfly who needed the protection from harm and danger!

I decided to use my mind and my voice instead of my muscles. I was remembering that, when I had been the striped cowboy riding a watermelon, I had scattered the girls in all directions by letting loose a series of wild loon calls, which sounded like a woman screaming or a wildcat with a trembling voice trying to scare the wits out of its prey.

So while I was still crouched in the shadows behind Poetry, I lifted my face to the sky and let loose six or seven bloodcurdling, high-pitched, trembling cries, making the loon call, the screech owl's screech, and a wolf's howl over and over again.

Poetry, catching on to my idea, joined in with a series of sounds like a young rooster learning to crow and a guinea hen's scrawny-necked squawking scream. That made me decide to also bark like a dog and let out a half-dozen long, wailing bawls like the kind Circus's dad's hound Old Bawler makes when she's on a red-hot coon trail.

We probably sounded like the midway of a county fair gone crazy, especially when all of a sudden Poetry, who could imitate almost every farm noise there is, started bawling like a calf and I went back to the loon call and the screech owl's screech. Then we began shaking the elm saplings we were under, making them sway as though a windstorm was blowing and a tornado would be there any minute.

Things happened pretty fast after that. The noise got even worse because, all mixed up with Dragonfly's sneezing and Poetry's and my eardrum-splitting noises were the different-pitched screams of the girls. All of a sudden there was a flurry of running feet, and in a flash the girls were tumbling over each other on their way up the slope, past the base of the leaning linden tree, and were gone! In my mind's eye I was watching them making a helter-skelter dash for the papaw bushes and their tents.

And that is how we practically saved Dragonfly's life that very first night of this story, which is only the beginning—and which made the mystery we were trying to solve seem more mysterious than ever.

5

Poor Dragonfly! I guess he never had been so frightened before in his life. Dog days are ragweed days—and nights, too—and he was not only sneezing but wheezing a little, which meant he might get an asthma attack any minute.

"The w–w–water—" he stammered and gestured behind him toward the spring.

Poetry and I were quickly out of our hiding place on our way to Dragonfly. *What*, I wondered, *is he trying to tell us about the watermelon?*

"M–m–my knife!" he spluttered. "It's in there—in the b–b–bottom of the pool!"

When I heard that, I *knew* he had been planning to plug the melon, which I was sure somebody had left there a few minutes ago. It didn't feel very good to have to believe one of our own gang had been mixed up with the stealing of melons from the Collins garden.

"Hurry!" Dragonfly wheezed. "G–g–get it for me! I've got to get home quick! My parents don't know where I am!"

Because all of us were in a hurry to get away from such a dangerous place for boys to be—which it certainly was, with a colony of bumble-bee-like girls on a temper spree—I exclaimed to Poetry, "Hold the flashlight for me. I'll get it!"

Poetry did, and I went to look for the knife, but I got an exclamation point in my mind for sure when I noticed there wasn't even one watermelon in the pool—neither the one I was sure somebody had just hoisted over the lip of the pool and lowered inside nor the long, beautiful one I had seen there myself, which had had the waxed-paper wadding in it and on which I had had a fierce, fast ride in the moonlight.

What on earth!

"C–c–come on! Hurry up!" Dragonfly cried. "I've got to get home before my father gets back from t–t–town. It's his knife, and I wasn't supposed to have it!"

I quickly shoved my stripeless pajama sleeve up to my shoulder. And while Poetry held the flashlight for me and Dragonfly shivered and wheezed and watched, I plunged my arm into that icy water. In a few seconds my fingers clasped the knife, and only a few seconds after that all of us were on our way up the incline.

At the top, we looked quick to see if the enemy had retreated, and they had—at least we didn't see or hear them. Then we skirted the rail fence and the evergreens and started on the run up the bayou, taking the way that most certainly wouldn't lead anywhere near the papaw bushes.

We would have looked very strange to most anybody—Poetry in his green-striped pajamas, I in my yellowish stripeless ones, and Dragonfly in his red stripes. That was the funny thing about it—that crooked-nosed, short-of-breath little guy being in his nightclothes, too.

When we asked him, "How come?" he panted back, "I didn't have time to dress. I had to get here and get back again before my father got home."

It wasn't a very satisfactory answer. His running around in the woods in his pajamas didn't make half as much sense as Poetry and I running around in ours did. It must have seemed absolutely nonsensical to those girl campers. They must have thought he and I were the same idiotic boy—which we most certainty weren't.

Dragonfly was going to explain further when his wheezy voice was interrupted by somebody in the direction of Bumblebee Hill calling my name and saying, *"Bill! Bill Collins! Where in the world are you?"*

"It's your father!" Poetry stopped stock-still and said.

It certainly was.

That big, half-worried, half-mad, thundery voice trumpeting down to us from the top of Bumblebee Hill was the well-known voice of Theodore Collins, my reddish brown mustached, bushy-eyebrowed father. What on earth was Dad doing out there waving his lantern and calling, "Bill Collins, where in the world are you?"

All of a sudden it seemed that, wherever I was, it was a good place not to be. It would be safer if I could take a fast shortcut through the woods and be fast asleep in the tent—or pretending to be—by the time Dad would give up looking for me and come back to the house. I could tell by the tone of his ear-deafening voice that whatever he was saying, he had already said it for the last time.

"Come on," I whispered to Poetry and Dragonfly, "let's get home quick. *Quick!*" And we lit out for my house by the shortcut that would miss Dad, who was still dodging along with his swinging lantern toward the bayou, still calling my name, and stopping every few yards to listen. If only Dragonfly could run faster, it would be easy, I thought.

Right then, to my surprise, Dad swung west and started on the run toward the spring. We quick dodged behind some chokecherry shrubs so as not to be seen. Then we scrambled up the hill and into the path made by boys' bare feet and in a jiffy reached the rail fence just across the road from the Collins gate and the walnut tree.

After that, in less than almost no time, we were inside the tent, Dragonfly puffing and wheezing because of his asthma, Poetry puffing because of his weight, and I just puffing.

But it wasn't any peaceful, quiet tent that we had come back to. Dragonfly was as wet as a drowned rat from having been dunked in the spring and was shivering with the cold, even on such a hot midsummer night!

We certainly had a problem on our hands. In fact the whole night was all messed up with problems. *Who* had crawled into our garden, picked one of our melons, slipped it into a burlap bag, dragged it on the end of a long plastic clothesline to a hole in the fence under the elderberry bushes, hoisted it into his car, and driven away with it? Who, quite a while later, had come rowing up the creek and left the melon in the spring? And how come there wasn't even one melon there a little later? What on earth was Dragonfly himself doing there? Was he actually looking for his knife, or had he had it with him all the time?

I felt the way I do sometimes on test day in school when the teacher gives me a piece of paper with seven or eight questions on it, quite a few of which I know I can't answer. Generally the paper has a note at the top that says, "Answer any five." But tonight's questions were worse. I'd certainly need to do a lot of studying to answer even *one* of them!

"I have got to get home and into bed before my father gets home from town and finds I'm not there!" Dragonfly whined.

"Why doesn't he know you are gone?" Poetry asked.

Dragonfly answered, "I climbed out of my bedroom window. I had to get to the spring to get the knife."

Then Dragonfly got what he thought was a good idea. "Let me have your red-striped pajamas until tomorrow, Bill." He was looking at me and, I guess, noticing I had on my yellow ones.

"I can't," I said. "They're all wet."

He was standing shivering in the light of Poetry's flashlight, and I was shivering, too—from all the excitement. Also I was still wondering how soon Dad would give up looking for us in the woods and come back to the tent. Dragonfly and I both had our fathers after us, I thought.

"Your red-striped pajamas are all wet?" Dragonfly exclaimed.

I answered, "Yes, they got dunked in the spring!" Of course, that didn't make sense to him.

We were all standing in the middle of the tent between the two cots, trying to decide what to do, when Poetry said, "I hear a telephone ringing somewhere."

I had already heard it. The sound was coming from our house through the open east window. Who, I wondered, would be calling the Collinses at this time of night? I knew that if Mom woke up and came downstairs to answer the phone, she'd be within a foot of the open window and she could hear anything we would say or do in the tent.

But nobody answered the phone. A second later it rang again. When still nobody answered, Poetry said, "Maybe your mother's out in the woods somewhere with your father. You'd better go answer it yourself."

I lifted the tent flap, sped out across the lawn to the board walk that leads from the back door to the pump, slipped into the house, worked my way through the dark kitchen to the living room, and hurried to the phone, my heart pounding from having hurried so fast.

"Hello," I said into the mouthpiece, making my voice sound as much like my mother's as I could.

There came screeching into my ear an excited woman's voice saying worriedly, "Hello, Mrs. Collins; I've been trying to get you. Is our boy, Roy, there?"

"Roy?" I asked. "Roy *who*?" I forgot for a second that Dragonfly's real name is Roy. The gang never called him that. He was just plain Dragonfly to us.

"Roy! My boy! He's not in his room, and I can't find him anywhere."

I didn't have time to tell her anything, because right that minute there was a voice whispering to me from outside the window, saying, "Who is it?"

I turned my face away from the telephone mouthpiece and said to Poetry, "It's Dragonfly's mother. She's afraid he's been kidnapped."

Then from behind me I heard footsteps in our dark house. Before I could wonder who it was, Mom's voice called from the bottom of the stairs, "What's going on down here?"

Mom certainly looked strange, standing there in the kitchen doorway in her nightgown and her hair all done up in curlers, which were shining in the light of the lamp she was carrying.

Right then Poetry's mischievous mind made

him say something that he must have thought was funny, but it wasn't because it made Mom gasp. His squawky, ducklike voice was almost like a ghost's voice coming loudly from just outside the window: "Everything's all right, Mrs. Collins. The phone rang, and Bill answered it, because your husband wasn't here but was out in the woods in his nightclothes racing around with a lantern and yelling wildly. The last we saw of him, he was running like an excited deer with hounds on his trail!"

To make matters worse, Dragonfly's mother was still on the phone and heard everything Poetry said. And she thought he had said that *Dragonfly* was running around in the woods with a lantern and yelling wildly with hounds on his trail. She gasped into the telephone the same kind of gasp Mom had just made.

"You want to talk to my mother?" I asked Mrs. Gilbert, glad for a chance to get out of the house. The second Mom took the receiver, I started to leave, and I would have if right that minute Charlotte Ann, in her bed in the downstairs bedroom, hadn't come to life with a frightened cry.

Mom told me to go in and see if Charlotte Ann had fallen out of bed.

In another second I would have been in the room where Charlotte Ann was, but first my eyes took a fleeting glance out the front screen door and across the road in the direction of the spring. There I saw a lighted lantern making crazy jiggling movements, which told me that Dad, who was carrying it, was running like a deer in the direction of our house. I knew that in another minute Theodore Collins would be over the rail fence, swishing past our mailbox, and sooner than anything would be there in the middle of all our excitement and wanting to know what was what and why.

Boy oh boy, you should have seen the way Dad flew into action the very minute he landed in his nightshirt and trousers in the middle of our brain-whirling trouble and excitement. But, for a father, he certainly didn't calm things down very fast—not the way a father is supposed to when he yells to everybody to calm down. Dad sometimes does that at our house when he thinks I, especially, am raising what he calls a "ruckus."

Of course, at first Dad didn't know I was inside the house trying to quiet Charlotte Ann or that Mom had gotten up and come downstairs and was talking to Dragonfly's mother on the phone trying to calm *her* down.

The first thing Dad noticed was Poetry, who by that time was in the middle of the yard not far from Dragonfly, who was not far from the tent. I could hear Dad's strong voice not far from the plum tree as he demanded of the whole Collins farm, "William Jasper Collins"—meaning me—"where on *earth* have you boys been? And *what* are you doing with those wet pajamas on again?" He was yelling that question at poor little red-striped-pajama-clad Dragonfly, who, of course, Dad must have thought was his own son.

Seeing and hearing Dad from the open window near the telephone, I yelled out to him, "I haven't got my red-striped pajamas on! They're still out on the line behind the grape arbor where you hung them yourself!"

You'd have thought Dad's ears could have told him that his son's voice had come from the house behind him and not from the tent in front of him. But Dad was looking at the boy in the shadow of the plum tree and in the sputtering light of his lantern. He barked back at Dragonfly, "Don't try to be funny!" and demanded an explanation.

All this time, Mom was using a soothing voice on Roy Gilbert's mother, while I was trying to quiet Charlotte Ann's half-scared-to-death voice.

And that was the way Dad's understanding of things began—and the way the next thirty minutes started.

What a night!

6

The excitement we were splashing around in—squawky-voiced, barrel-shaped Poetry; red-striped-pajama-clad Dragonfly; nightgown-dressed Mom; crying Charlotte Ann; my confused father; and his actual son—couldn't last forever, and this didn't!

In not too long a while, Dad began to get things clear in his usually bright mind, as Poetry and I managed to squeeze in a few words of explanation. We kept some of the mystery to ourselves to talk over with the gang tomorrow, when we would have our meeting at the Little Jim Tree at the bottom of Bumblebee Hill. (That's the name we had given the tree under which Little Jim had killed the fierce, mad old mother bear.)

It seemed we should tell Dad and Mom why Poetry and I had been running around in a beautiful moonlit night in our nightclothes, though. So, as soon as we could, we explained about the watermelon in the burlap bag and the noisy old car racing down the lane and coming back a little later.

Dad really fired up when I mentioned how the thief had managed to get the watermelon through the fence. "You mean somebody cut a hole in my new woven wire fence!" he half shouted. "We'll go down there right now and have a look at it!" He was more angry, it seemed, that his fence had been cut than that one of our watermelons had been stolen.

Dragonfly broke in then, saying, "I've got to get home."

The way he said it made me wonder if he knew all about the whole thing and just wanted to get away from us.

Mom decided what we were going to do first. She said, "I promised Roy's mother we'd drive him home right away."

That did seem the best thing to do, and in a little while all of us, including Mom and Charlotte Ann, were in our car driving up the road to Dragonfly's house.

It took quite a few minutes for Mom and Dad and me to calm Dragonfly's mother down —she was so upset. I helped as much as I could, taking as much blame as I thought would be safe. But I *didn't* want his mother to punish that spindle-legged, crooked-nosed little guy for doing practically nothing, which it looked like maybe she was excited enough and nervous enough to do.

"You know how boys are," Mom said. "They get ideas of things they want to do, and they think afterward."

Dad helped a little by saying, "Even our own son does unpredictable things once in a while. Isn't that right, Bill?"

It was too dark there in the shadow of the big cedar tree that grows close to Dragonfly's side door for Dad to see me frown. But I decided to look up the word *unpredictable* in our dictionary as soon as I got a chance, just to see what kind of things I did once in a while. I hoped they weren't as bad as such a long word made them sound.

"It's my fault he got his pajamas all wet," I thought it was safe to say to Dragonfly's worried mother. Then I told her a little about the girls at the spring and how they probably thought Dragonfly was me. I *didn't* tell her I thought maybe her innocent son was mixed up in our watermelon mystery, or she might have had insomnia that night even worse than another boy's mother.

From Dragonfly's house we drove back toward ours, turned into the lane that goes down the south side of our farm, and stopped at the place in the fence where the elderberry bushes were. It was the very same place where not more than two hours ago the noisy oldish car had been parked.

When Dad's flashlight showed him the hole in the fence under the elderberry bushes, he was as angry as I have ever seen him get. He just stood there at the side of our car, with the moonlight shining on his stern face, his jaw muscles working, and I knew every other muscle in his body was tense.

"It's hard to believe anybody would be *that* mean," he said.

"Bob Till is mean enough to do anything," I answered.

But Mom stopped me before I could say another word. "You're *not* to say that!" she ordered me. "We're going to give that boy a chance. We're *not* going to believe he did this until we have proof."

"How much more proof do we want?" I asked. "We saw his car parked here. We saw the watermelon being dragged in the gunnysack along the fence right over there. And we actually saw it being dragged through this hole and hoisted into the car. And we saw him drive away —Poetry and I both did."

"Did you count your melons?" Mom asked. "Were there any missing?"

"Were there any—" I stopped. I didn't even know how many melons we *had*. I'd never bothered to count them. Those smaller melons hadn't seemed as important to me as Ida had, because they had grown from ordinary watermelon seed and not from the packet of special seed from the state experiment station.

The only way I could know for sure if any were taken would be to look all over the patch to see if there were any oblong indentations in the ground where a melon *had* been.

"All right," I said, "I'll find out right now. I *know* there was a watermelon in that gunnysack. I felt it with my own hands, and it was long and round and hard."

Dad let me have his flashlight, and I crawled through the fence and started looking around all over the garden to see if there were any melons missing. I made a beeline straight for Ida's vine to be sure she was there and all right.

Poetry wanted to go with me, but he couldn't get through the small hole in the fence. "At least that proves *he* didn't do it," Dad said grimly.

Poetry answered, "If I'd been cutting a hole in a nice new fence, I'd have made it large enough for a man my size to get through." He was trying to be funny even at a time like that!

In only a few barefoot minutes, I was standing beside the circular trough in which Ida's vine was growing, and my flashlight was making a circular arc all around the place while my eyes were looking for Ida herself.

And then, all of a sudden, I felt myself get hot inside, and I heard at the same time my excited, angry voice almost screaming back across the moonlit watermelon patch to Mom and Dad and Charlotte Ann and Poetry, *"She's gone! Somebody's sneaked in while we were away and stolen her!"*

There in front of my tear-blurred eyes was a long, smooth indentation in the ground where for the last eighty-five days—which is how long it takes to mature a melon—Ida Watermelon Collins had made her home. I was all mixed up with temper and sobs and doubled-up fists and was ready to explode.

Ida was gone! Ida had been stolen! My *prize watermelon!* The mother of my next year's watermelon children and the grandmother of my year-after-next's watermelon grandchildren —and my college education.

I tell you, there were a lot of what Dad called "stormy emotions" whirling around in our minds when, a little later, the five of us got back into the car and drove on down the lane in the direction of the Sugar Creek schoolhouse, so as to find a place in the road wide enough to turn around in.

We talked a lot and tried to make plans, especially Poetry and I in the backseat. I simply couldn't understand my parents' attitude. There was Dad's fence with an ugly hole in it, and Ida was missing, and yet he was now very calm and very set in his mind about what not to do.

"Like your mother says, Bill, we don't *know* that Bob did it. It won't cost much to repair the fence, and next year we'll raise another melon that'll be even bigger and better."

I stormed awhile there in the backseat until I got strict orders from both my parents to calm down. Mom made it easier for me to do that by adding, as we pulled up to our mailbox, "We're Christians. We don't take revenge on people. We're going to commit this thing to the Lord and see what good He will bring out of it."

It was quite a while before things were quiet around the Collins farm that night, with Dad and Mom and Charlotte Ann in the house and Poetry and I in our hot cots in the tent under the plum tree.

Tomorrow, when the gang got together, we'd decide what to do. It seemed, though, that Mom's attitude was going to be like a lasso on a rodeo steer to keep me from doing what I really wanted to do, which was to hunt up Bob Till himself and face him with the question of what he had done with my watermelon.

"Listen," I hissed all of a sudden to Poetry in his cot. Before he could answer, I went on, "If we can find out what happened to the melon, maybe we can still get the seed from it. Anybody he sold it to wouldn't eat the *seeds*."

At the breakfast table the next morning, Dad's prayer was a little longer than usual, and it seemed sort of meant for me to hear. Right in the middle of it, while Charlotte Ann, in the crook of Mom's arm, was wriggling and squirming and reaching both hands and fussing to get started eating, Dad said, ". . . And bless with a very special blessing those who have sinned against themselves and against You by breaking the commandment 'You shall not steal.' Help us to love them and to show them by our lives that the Christian life is the only truly satisfying life. Keep us under Your control . . ."

That last request bothered me a little because it seemed I wanted to be under my own control all day—and that if I was going to be under anybody else's control, I might not get to help teach Bob Till, or whoever it was who had cut the hole in Dad's new fence and stolen that watermelon, a good old-fashioned lesson by giving him a licking.

Mom's buckwheat pancakes were the best Poetry had ever tasted, he told her—which was probably his excuse for tasting so many of them. He certainly knew how to make Mom's eyes twinkle. Mom liked boys so well, anyway. In fact all the boys of the Sugar Creek Gang liked Mom so well that they stopped at our house every chance they got just to make her eyes twinkle while they ate some of her cookies or a piece of one of her pies.

She surprised us all right then by saying, "Last night while I couldn't sleep for a while, I got to thinking about whoever took your melon and cut the hole in the fence, and it seemed the Lord wanted me to pray for him or them. I feel so sorry for boys who do things like that."

Mom sighed heavily, and I noticed that her eyes had a faraway expression in them. Just looking at her made me think it would be pretty hard for me to be a bad boy as long as I had such a wonderful mother.

After breakfast and before we left the table, we passed around what we call the "Bread Box," which is a small box of cards, each one with a Bible verse printed on it. And do you know what? Just as it had been when Dad prayed, I felt like a frisky young steer that has just been lassoed, because the card I picked out of the box when it was passed to me had on it, *"Love your enemies, do good to those who hate you . . . pray for those who mistreat you."*

When I got through reading my verse aloud, as we all do every time, I looked across the table toward Dad, and his gray green eyes were looking straight into mine. He had a half grin on his face when he said, just as if there wasn't anybody else in the room, "Your watermelon and my fence!" I could tell by the expression in his voice that he had been lassoed, too!

Poetry and I managed to get through the morning all right, but it was hard to wait until two o'clock in the afternoon. We did quite a little work around the place, though, such as helping Mom with the dishes, helping Dad with the chores, and running a few errands for each of them.

Once we stopped in the middle of the barnyard while I pointed out to Poetry the boss hen of our whole flock, the one Dad has named Cleopatra. Cleopatra is a very proud, high-combed, very pretty white leghorn. Like all boss hens in a hen flock, she could peck all the other hens anytime she wanted to, but not a one of them ever dared to peck her back. She had already proved to them who was boss by giving every one of them a licking one at a time.

"We've got a boss hen, too," Poetry told me as we stood watching Cleopatra proudly lifting her yellow feet and strutting around to show how important she was.

"We have a *second* boss too. She pecks every other hen except the boss hen, and Cleopatra is the only one that can peck her," I told him. Anybody who knows anything about what Dad calls the "social life of a flock of hens" knows that is the way they live and get along with each other. At the very bottom of the social ladder in the Collins chicken yard is a bedraggled-looking hen Mom has named Marybelle Elizabeth. She gets pecked by every other hen in the barnyard and can never peck *any* of them back.

We liked Marybelle Elizabeth, though. She was one of the best-laying hens we had, even though in a fight she wasn't any good at defending herself and she always ate her lunch alone when all the others were through.

I was standing beside Poetry near our garden fence, watching Marybelle while she foraged around by herself as though she didn't have a friend in the world. I was feeling very sorry for her and thinking how lonely a life she had to live and how she had to take all the unfair things the other hens did to her and couldn't ever fight back.

Poetry moseyed on toward the house then, and I kept on standing not more than fifteen feet from Marybelle. "Here, Marybelle," I comforted her, "don't you feel too bad. I live a kind of henpecked life myself." Taking a handful of corn from my pocket, I tossed it to her. She lifted her head high, twisted her neck in every direction as if she wondered how come anybody wanted to be kind to *her*, then started gobbling up the kernels of corn as fast as she could.

"Attagirl," I said to her. "Go to it!"

Pretty soon Mom called to us that lunch was ready, and pretty soon after lunch—and after Poetry and I had offered to help Mom with the dishes and she had surprised us by letting us—it was time for the gang to meet under the Little Jim Tree.

It was the nicest dog-days day I ever saw.

The heat waves danced above the fields, and short-horned grasshoppers sprang up along the sunny path as Poetry and I moseyed along, not wanting to run and get hot on such a hot day. I still felt kind of sad because of the watermelon and also because our boys' world had been invaded by a flock of girl campers. Girls in our woods would be a lasso on a boy's fun. He couldn't go racing wildly among the trees, playing leapfrog and yelling and whooping it up like a banshee, because he would be afraid they would think he *was* a banshee.

As I was saying, the short-horned grasshoppers were springing up all along the path, making their funny little rattling sounds during the short time they were in the air. The rattling stopped the very second they landed, which they generally did only a few yards from where they took off. Butterflies of a half-dozen families were tossing themselves about in the air above the wild rosebushes and here and there and everywhere in the yellow afternoon.

"Look at that!" Poetry exclaimed. "There goes a milkweed butterfly! I've got to have him for my collection!" And he started after it.

But I stopped him with: *"Quiet! The girls will hear you!"*

He stopped and scowled, and the beautiful monarch butterfly swung proudly away in the air, starting to stop every now and then, and not doing it but lifting itself on the breeze and floating away to another place.

It wouldn't be long until fall now, I

thought, when all the monarchs in the Sugar Creek territory would gather themselves into flocks the way blackbirds and crows do. Before winter they would migrate south, flying all the way down to the bottom of the United States and even into Mexico or South America. Then, next spring, they would be back at Sugar Creek to lay their eggs on the milkweeds that grow in the fencerows or wherever a farmer doesn't cut them down.

The larva that hatches from the milkweed, or monarch, butterfly is one of the prettiest a boy ever sees. It's a long, greenish yellow caterpillar with black rings around it all along its body from its head to its tail. But it is hard to tell which end is its head, because it has two short black horns on each end of itself.

You can see a yellow-and-black Monarch larva hanging from a milkweed leaf most anytime in the late summer, if you stop and look close enough.

Dragonfly was the only one of the gang who didn't come to our meeting that day, and Poetry and I thought we knew why.

We all plumped ourselves down on the grass under the Little Jim Tree and relaxed awhile, each of us lying in a different direction, as we nearly always do. Big Jim looked around at the rest of us, letting his stern eyes stop on each of our faces for a flash of a second—Poetry's round, mischievous face; Little Jim's mouselike, innocent face; Circus's monkey-shaped face; and my freckle-faced face.

Big Jim's own face was more sober than it is sometimes, and I noticed that the almost-mustache on his upper lip was *really* almost there now. If it should keep on growing as fast as it had the last two or three years, pretty soon he would actually have to start shaving.

"Anybody know where Dragonfly is?" Big Jim asked.

And Poetry answered, "He had asthma last night. Maybe his mother wouldn't let him come today."

Big Jim's serious face probably meant he was remembering his resolution not to fight Bob Till anymore unless he was forced to in self-defense. Of course, if Bob himself started a fight, we'd have to defend ourselves.

I got an idea then, so I said, "Bob Till has already started a fight by stealing our watermelons last night. That's the same as whamming me in the stomach, because that's where the watermelons would have been if I had eaten them. And since he's already *started* a fight, I've got a right to defend myself, haven't I?"

"It's not the same," Big Jim said grimly, his jaw muscles still working. His fists were doubled up, though, I noticed, and I could see he didn't like the lasso with which he had lassoed himself.

Little Jim spoke up then. "How would we feel in Sunday school tomorrow if Bob came in with a black eye?"

I looked into that little guy's face and saw how innocent he was. He was so tenderhearted that he'd probably even hate to swat a fly—and wouldn't if he didn't think the fly needed to be swatted.

Right then was when I noticed for the first time the manila envelope Little Jim had brought with him. It looked about five inches wide and nine inches long and had something in it. I couldn't tell what it was and didn't get to find out until later in the afternoon.

Little Jim's question took some of the fight out of me, because I knew Bob *had* to be in church tomorrow. That was one of the things the judge who had put him on probation had said he had to do—go to Sunday school and church at least once every Sunday for a whole year.

I spoke up then with a half-mischievous voice. "The judge told him he had to go every Sunday unless he is sick and unable to. He might *not* be able to if—"

"Stop!" Big Jim cut in. "The thing is not funny!"

Not a one of us said a word more for a minute. Then Big Jim told us in a serious voice, "We can't let Bob break his parole. If he does, he'll have to go to reform school for from one to ten years, and we wouldn't want that."

"Hasn't he already broken parole by stealing my watermelons?" I asked.

Again Big Jim cut in on me almost savagely, "You don't *know* that. It could have been somebody else."

"It was *his* car," I countered. "I'd know it anywhere."

Just thinking about that burlap bag with the stolen watermelon in it and Ida herself being gone stirred me all up inside again, and I was in a whirlwind of a mood to do something about it. I thought about poor old Marybelle Elizabeth out by our garden fence, all alone at the very bottom of our chicken yard's social ladder, and how she had to take all the pecks of all the other hens and didn't dare fight back. I felt sorry for her having to live such a hen-pecked life. Right that minute, if I had been Marybelle, I'd have felt in a mood to start in licking the feathers off every other hen in the whole Sugar Creek territory.

But we couldn't just lie around and talk all afternoon and *do* nothing. *Nothing* is something a boy can do for only a few minutes at a time, anyway.

"Let's go swimming," Little Jim suggested.

"Can't," I said crossly. "We don't have our swimsuits."

"Swimsuits!" Circus exclaimed. "Who ever heard of the Sugar Creek Gang using swim trunks in our own swimming hole!"

Nobody ever had, because our swimming hole was quite a way up the creek and was well protected on both sides by bushes and shrubbery. Besides, nobody lived anywhere near the place.

"There are guests in our woods," Big Jim reminded Circus.

And my sad heart told me he was right. We *couldn't* go swimming.

"Girls!" Poetry grunted grouchily.

He got shushed by Big Jim, who asked, "They're human beings, aren't they?"

"Are they?" Poetry asked in an innocent voice.

Big Jim sighed, looked around at all of us again, and said, "Little Jim here has something he has to do this afternoon, and it could be a little dangerous. He might need our help. You guys want to go along with him and me?"

I said, "I am going to do something dangerous myself before the afternoon is over, but I don't suppose any of you would care to go with me. You don't care whether my prize watermelon was stolen or not. But *I* do, and I'm going to do something about it!"

My words sounded hot in my ears and made me a little braver than I had been. They reminded me of Marybelle Elizabeth at the bottom of our chicken yard's social ladder, living a henpecked life and not daring to fight back at all at anytime.

"What you going to do?" Circus asked. "I'm willing to go along and help save your life if you need any help."

"Yeah, what *are* you going to do?" Poetry asked me.

I answered, "First, I'm going down to the spring to see if Ida is there. If she's not, I'm going down to the bridge, and across it, and straight to Bob Till's house, and ask him straight out if he knows anything about a watermelon thief."

I caught Big Jim and Little Jim's eyes meeting and thought I saw some kind of message pass between them.

"You guys don't have to go along if you don't want to," I said, beginning to feel a little less brave, now that it seemed I was about to do more than just talk and was actually going to do what I said I was going to do.

"We can't let you be killed," Circus said. "Maybe we *all* ought to go along!"

Pretty soon we were on our way—to the spring first, of course. As we moved grimly along, I noticed my teeth were clenched, my lips were pressed together in a straight line, my eyebrows were down. I was remembering last night's ridiculous ride on the melon in the spring reservoir, the screaming girls, and especially what had happened in our melon patch near the elderberry bushes.

But right in the front of my mind's eye was the oblong indentation in the sandy loam where Ida Watermelon Collins had spent all the eighty-five days of her life from a tiny quarter-of-an-inch-long green baby to the huge, dark green watermelon she now was, if she was. Where, I asked myself, was Ida now?

Maybe she was in the spring reservoir. Maybe whoever stole her had sold her to the Girl Scouts. When we got there, would we run into a flock of perfumed guests, and would they recognize a zebra who had changed his color and shape since last night?

Well, we didn't find any girls there, and we didn't find any watermelon, either. All there was in the big cement pool was a glass fruit jar filled with butter and a half-dozen cartons of milk, and there were girls' shoe tracks all around the place.

There weren't any boys' tracks—not even barefoot ones.

Big Jim wanted to look around where the boat had been moored, so we all gathered in a huddle by the maple tree, keeping as quiet as we could so that, if anyone did come to the spring, we wouldn't be seen or heard.

Little Jim slipped out of our huddle and began nosing around over by the board fence where last night Poetry and I had crawled through in such a hurry.

"Hey, everybody!" all of a sudden Little Jim's excited, mouselike voice squeaked to us. "Look what I found! A note of some kind!"

He was holding up a piece of paper.

I remembered then that that was the exact place where Poetry and I had been when we had unfolded the waxed paper that said on it "Eat more Eatmore Bread."

Poetry's and my eyes met, and we grunted to each other.

"That's only an old bread wrapper. We threw it away last night," I said to Little Jim.

"You shouldn't have," Little Jim answered. He came loping over to where we were with the happiest grin on his face you ever saw. He held the waxed paper out to us. "Look! There's a note inside it. See!" he cried.

You could have knocked me over with a watermelon seed, I was so astonished. The waxed paper said, "Eat more Eatmore Bread," all right, but as plain as day there *was* something sealed between two layers of the paper. A thought hit my mind with a thud—there was something very important on that paper!

"Let's get out of here quick," Big Jim said. Taking the paper and ordering, "Follow me!" he started on the run up the path that led through the forest of giant ragweed toward the old swimming hole.

Zippety-zip-zip, plop-plop-plop went my bare feet on the cool, damp, winding path through the ragweed, following along with the rest of the gang.

But the minute we reached the place where we had had so many happy times each summer, we heard voices from up the creek.

"Girls!" Circus exclaimed disgustedly. "Let's get out of here!"

I looked in the direction the sounds came from and saw a boat with three or four girls in it. Well, in less than a firefly's fleeting flash, we were up and gone again, scooting through the rows of tall corn and headed for the east end of the bayou.

"We'll have our meeting in the graveyard," Big Jim said. "They'll be afraid to come there."

7

In almost less time than it has taken me to write these few paragraphs, we were in the cemetery at the top of Bumblebee Hill, sprawled out on the grass near Sarah Paddler's tombstone—the one that has the carved hand on it with the forefinger pointing toward the sky, the one with the words that say, "There is rest in heaven."

Every time we had a meeting there, I would read those words and look at the other tombstone, exactly the same size, which had on it Old Man Paddler's name and the date the old man was born, with a blank place after it—meaning he was still alive and nobody would put on the date of his death until after his funeral.

Also I would always remember that that kind, long-whiskered man was an honest-to-goodness Christian, who loved the heavenly Father and His only Son. He trusted in the Savior for the forgiveness of his sins. So I was sure that, when he *did* die, his soul would go to heaven, where his wife, Sarah, and his two boys already were—and the whole family would be together again.

That old cemetery was certainly an interesting place and was very pretty. I hoped that nobody would ever try to make it look like the well-kept cemeteries around the county. It'd be nice if people would let the wild rosebushes and the chokecherries and the sumac and the elderberries and the wild grapevines keep on growing there. Of course, it would be all right to keep the weeds away from the different markers and to keep the grass cut, but I liked the little brown paths that wound around from one to the other. And it always seemed that God was there in a special way.

You get a kind of a sad-happy feeling in your heart when you think about Him, when all your sins are forgiven, and when you and your parents like each other. It seems as if maybe He likes boys especially well, because He made such a nice boys' world for them to live in.

There was purple vervain growing all over the place and tall mullein stalks. And already the sumac was turning red. I hadn't any more than thought all these things, when from behind the sumac on the other side of Sarah Paddler's tall tombstone I heard a long-tailed sneeze and knew Dragonfly was there. A moment later he came pouting into the little circular open place we were in, saying, "How come you didn't wait for me?"

He looked a little guilty, I thought, as, panting and wheezing a little, he plumped himself down on the ground between Poetry and me.

Everything was so quiet for a minute that he must have guessed we had been talking about him. "Are the—are the girls still camping up in the woods?" he asked. I knew he was remembering last night's dunking in the spring and also probably never would forget it.

There was an interrogatory sentence in my mind right that minute. So I exploded at Dragonfly, "What were you doing in the middle of the night down there at the spring?"

My question probably sounded pretty saucy to him.

"I went to get my knife," he said. "I was there getting a drink yesterday afternoon when a whole flock of girls came storming down and scared me so bad I dropped my knife. I was so scared I ran home. It was my dad's knife, and he was coming home before midnight, and I didn't want him to know I had it, so I sneaked back to get it, and—"

Another of my mystery balloons had burst. Poetry and I looked at each other and shrugged. That let Dragonfly out. He hadn't had anything to do with stealing watermelons. He was as innocent as a lamb. I sighed a big sigh of relief, though. It felt good to get all that suspicion out of my mind and to have Dragonfly with us again.

We crowded around Big Jim then to see what was between the layers of the bread wrapper.

"It's a map!" Little Jim exclaimed in his squeaky voice.

It was a crude drawing made with purple pencil. That was the first thing I noticed—that it had been made with purple pencil. The drawing looked like a map of the Sugar Creek territory itself. In fact, it was a very *good* map of the gang's playground and had the names of important places on it—names that only somebody living in our neighborhood would know about. There were a few names that it seemed only the gang itself might know, such as Bumblebee Hill, the Black Widow Stump, and the Little Jim Tree.

My mind cringed when I realized that maybe whoever had drawn the map was one of our own gang—maybe one of us who, right that minute, were in a football-style huddle in the cemetery.

Then Poetry noticed something I hadn't. "Look at that red X, would you? Wonder what that means?"

I squeezed in between Poetry and Dragonfly and looked. And there it was, a very small red X with a red circle around it in the upper lefthand corner of the page. I could tell that the red X and the red circle were marking a spot on the other side of the creek just below the big Sugar Creek bridge.

Big Jim must have been thinking the same thoughts I was, because right that second he said, "Who outside our gang knows the name of the tree where Little Jim killed the bear?"

Poetry rolled himself into a sitting position and grunted himself to his feet. Trying to make his voice sound like a detective's, he said, "All right, everybody. Don't a one of you leave this room—this cemetery, I mean. One of you in this circle is a watermelon thief. One of you drew this map!"

Before anybody could have stopped him, he was firing one question after another at us. The first one was, "Who among us has a purple pencil? You, Bill?"

"No sir," I said.

I was surprised that Big Jim let Poetry keep on with his questions, but he did, and pretty soon Poetry had asked us a half-dozen others, such as, which of us ate Eatmore Bread at home, what kind of clotheslines did our mothers use—rope or plastic—and did any of us smoke? Of course, the last question was a foolish one as far as the gang was concerned, but I knew why he had asked it. He was remembering the man in the boat who, last night, had lit a cigar or cigarette with a match or a lighter.

Poetry was looking as dignified as any roly-poly boy with mussed-up hair and mischievous eyes can look. He was all set to keep on talking and asking questions when Big Jim interrupted.

"Look, all of you! There's only one other person—well, two—who might know the names we've given to the important places around here. One is Little Tom Till, and the other is his big brother, Bob."

I don't know why I hadn't thought of Tom before. The very second Big Jim mentioned his name, I remembered that Tom was very good in art at school. In fact, he got better grades in it than any of the rest of us. For some reason, though, I didn't like the idea of thinking that

Tom was guilty of making the map. He wasn't *exactly* a member of our gang yet. He hadn't been meeting with the gang lately, because his brother didn't want him to and Tom was very much afraid of his big brother's big fists. But we all felt he belonged to us anyway.

"The thing for us to do," Big Jim interrupted my thoughts to say, "is to do what Bill suggests—go straight to their house and ask them point-blank what they know about this map and whether they've been stealing watermelons."

That is what we decided to do, but Big Jim cautioned us to watch our words so as not to stir up Bob's temper.

"Remember, he will be in church tomorrow—and in our class."

I remembered it all the way.

Our faces were set as we left the cemetery and walked down the slope of Bumblebee Hill. We passed the Little Jim Tree and went on to the spring again, then moved cautiously through the woods toward the rail fence that bordered the north road, keeping our distance from the papaw bushes on the way. Dragonfly managed to sneeze several times just as we were parallel with the Girl Scout camp, which proved that his mind as well as his nose was allergic to perfume, because he certainly wasn't close enough to their camp to smell any!

"Girls aren't anything to be sneezed at," Poetry was smart enough to say to Dragonfly, and Dragonfly sneezed again.

At the rail fence, we went through or under

or over the different rails, whichever different ones of us decided to do, and quickly were on our way across the bridge in the direction of the Tills' house.

The minute we reached the other side of the bridge, Little Jim cried suddenly, "There's the boat I bet they used last night!"

I looked downstream in the direction he was pointing and saw the red stern of a rowboat half hidden under some low-hanging willow branches.

A thousand shivers started racing up and down my spine when I realized that our mystery was coming to more life even than it had come to last night when we had seen the boat stopping at the spring.

At that very same instant I saw, half hidden among the trees, the forest green roof of a tent. *What on earth?* I thought.

Not only was there a flock of *girls* camping near the papaw bushes in the woods above the bridge, but here, on the other side of the creek and below the bridge, somebody else was camping! I was remembering last night and the mysterious something or other I had seen somebody carry to the spring from a boat. This very same boat, maybe!

Poetry beside me remarked, "There's where the woman lives—the one who was smoking the cigarette last night."

"There's where the *man* lives, you mean," I disagreed.

Beside the tent was a gunmetal gray pickup

truck that looked as though it was maybe ten or fifteen years old. At almost the same instant, there was the sound of a motor roaring to life, and right away the truck was moving. It went backward first, then swung left and began bumping along the little lane toward the highway.

"Quick, everybody!" Big Jim ordered. "Down the embankment and under the bridge!"

We obeyed Big Jim like soldiers taking orders from a captain in a battle. In only a few lightning-fast seconds, we were all crouching on a narrow strip of shore underneath the north end of the bridge. We got there just in time, too, because soon we heard the truck's wheels on the board floor above us. And that was that!

As soon as the truck was across the bridge, we decided it would be a good idea to look around a little, just to see if we could find any "clues," as Poetry was always saying.

We followed the narrow footpath that skirts the shore and is bordered on either side with willows and ragweeds, just like the path on our own side of the creek.

Pretty soon we came to within twenty-five feet of the boat and the green tent.

"Hello, there!" Big Jim called. "Anybody home?"

There wasn't any answer from anybody.

"Hello! I say, *hello!*" Big Jim called again several times, and still there wasn't any reply.

Though it wouldn't be right to trespass on

somebody's campground, we knew we wouldn't be doing anything wrong if we just walked in the path that belonged to everybody, anyway, past the place where the boat was moored.

Then we were there, and what to my wondering eyes should appear but out in the middle of the boat a gunnysack—an actual, honest-to-goodness gunnysack. It had something in it that was fat and long and—

"Hey," I said to the gang, "look! There's another watermelon! In a gunnysack!"

"You're crazy," Poetry answered. "That's not a watermelon. That's a water jug!"

Well, to my very sad disappointment, Poetry was right. There was a great big water jug like the kind we use at the Sugar Creek threshing time, wrapped round and round with a gunnysack tied on with twine.

I remembered that many a time I had carried drinking water to Dad from our iron pitcher pump out across the barnyard to whatever field he was in at the time. First, I would soak a burlap bag in cold water. If you do that to a burlap bag, it will keep the water in the jug cool for quite a long time.

"That," Poetry said, "is what the woman in the boat last night was getting at the spring. She carried an empty jug to the spring, let it down into the water until it was filled, and then carried it back again."

"I still want to know who drew a map and put it in that watermelon," I said crossly. "And *where* is Ida!"

After Big Jim had called, "Hello," a few more times and nobody had answered, we decided to see if we could find any honest-to-goodness clues, but we wouldn't go inside the tent.

"Look at that, would you?" Poetry exclaimed, the minute we were on the other side of the tent. "See that clothesline hanging between those two trees?" Most of us had already seen it. It was a brand-new plastic line stretching from a small maple near the tent to the trunk of an ash that grew about thirty feet away, close to a field of very tall corn. Hanging on the line were two or three pairs of pants, the kind women and girls wear. Also there were several kinds of women's different-colored clothes.

We didn't have time to try to make up our minds what to do next, because all of a sudden there was a clattering of the boards of the Sugar Creek bridge. It was the truck coming back.

"Quick, everybody!" Big Jim exclaimed. "Let's get out of here!"

And out of there we got, scurrying like six scared cottontails into the tall corn. We didn't stop running until we knew we were far enough away so that we couldn't be seen by anybody, not even if she dropped down on her hands and knees and looked beneath the drooping corn blades in our direction.

"I guess this lets Bob and Tom out," Circus said.

It had also knocked the daylights out of my mystery.

"But what about the burlap bag with the watermelon in it—the one that was being dragged through our watermelon patch last night?" I asked.

"It was *dark* out there, wasn't it?" Circus asked. "You couldn't tell whether it was a watermelon or a water jug."

"But I felt it with my two hands, and it was long and round and—"

"A water jug is long and round," Little Jim's mouselike voice squeaked.

"But this one in our watermelon patch didn't have any *spout* on it," I protested, feeling my mystery house falling and crashing all around me. "And why was it in our watermelon patch?"

"How do you know it didn't have a spout? You didn't feel both *ends*, did you? You just felt it in the middle," Poetry argued back. "And besides," he went on in a talkative hurry, "your other pump wasn't more than twenty feet away when we first saw it. Somebody was just helping himself to some drinking water."

I felt my jaw muscles tightening with anger. I knew—*knew*—that what had been in that burlap bag last night was a watermelon. Besides, why would anybody want to get drinking water secretly like that?

I quickly asked that question out loud and got a quick answer from Poetry, whose detective-like mind was certainly alert that day. "Sugar Creek water isn't safe to drink for anything except a fish in dog days. Look at all that green scum floating out there."

He was probably right, but his answer didn't tell me *why* whoever wanted the water didn't go right straight to any member of the Sugar Creek Gang's parents and ask for a jug of water in the daytime.

"But somebody *did* take my prize watermelon!" I protested. "Ida couldn't just get up and walk away. Somebody had to carry or drag her."

And a second later, Poetry started to say a little jingle we'd heard him use quite a few times. It was:

> "I proposed to Ida.
> Ida refused;
> I'da won my Ida if I'da used . . ."

"Stop!" I ordered him and started to say something else. But I got stopped myself by Big Jim, making me swallow my words and my temper. But still I knew I was right. The whole thing was as plain as a dog-days day to anybody with half a mind, and it looked as if maybe I was the only one of us who had that.

That was as far as any of us got to say or think right then, because from the direction of the tent I heard a car door slam. I knew it was the truck, and my mind was busy trying to imagine who had probably climbed out of it.

"Do you suppose it's anybody we know?" Dragonfly asked. Then he sneezed and grabbed his nose with his right hand to stop another sneeze that was already getting ready to explode.

For a few anxious seconds we all lay there in the nice clean dust of the cornfield, listening and thinking and trying to decide what to do, if anything. Even though I was worrying because of the mystery, I was hearing and actually enjoying the sound of the husky, rusty rustle of the corn blades in the very light breeze that was blowing. I could see big, white cumulus clouds hanging in the lazy afternoon sky and the shimmering green leaves at the top of the cottonwood tree farther down the shore. I even noticed a lazy crow loafing along in the sky as if he didn't have a worry in the world.

It wouldn't be long before fall would be here, I thought, and that lonely old crow would join about five hundred of his black-feathered friends and spend half the day every day for a while, cawing and cawing in his hoarse voice, keeping it up and keeping it up, hour after hour in the bare trees. One of the dreariest things a farm boy ever sees in the autumn is a forlorn-looking crow flapping his sad wings above the frosty cornfields.

Nearly every summer there is a crow's nest in the top of the old pine tree on the other side of the creek near the mouth of the branch. About all a pair of crow parents ever do to make a nest for their crow children to be hatched in is to build a rough platform of sticks, some large and some small, and line it with strips of bark from the cedar trees. Then the mother crow, who is just as black as her husband, though her feathers don't shine as brightly, lays from four to seven eggs that are the color of green dust with little brown spots on them.

Crows are always scattering themselves over the new cornfields in the spring, digging down into the rows where the grain has been planted, and gobbling up the grain before it has a chance to grow. Of course, any farm boy knows a crow also eats May beetles and grasshoppers and cutworms and caterpillars and even mice. He is also a thief. *But he doesn't use a plastic clothesline to help him get what he wants.*

Just thinking that brought my mind back to the cornfield we were lying in right that minute.

My thoughts got there just in time to hear Big Jim say to me, "Bill, you and Poetry tell us once more all you know about everything from the beginning up to now."

Poetry and I did, rehearsing to the gang what we had seen at the spring on our first trip—the plugged watermelon with the folded waxed paper in it; the long dark thing we had seen being dragged through the melon patch, which at first I had thought was some kind of wild animal running; and the car that clattered down the lane and back again. We told them about the hole in the fence and the watermelon being pulled through—or the water jug, whichever it was—and hoisted into the car. Then we told about Poetry's and my trip back to the spring again, the mystery man or woman in the boat, and Dragonfly's coming for his knife and getting dunked by the girls.

"Don't forget the perfume," Dragonfly said, "and the pine-scented paper and the map and—" And then he quickly grabbed his nose just in time to stop another sneeze.

"And the red letter X," Little Jim put in.

Big Jim unfolded the map again, and we crowded around him to study it.

There was only one person I knew who could draw a map as neat as that. "We'd better see Tom about this," I said. "Here, let me have it. I'm the one who took it out of the melon in the first place."

I was surprised when Big Jim actually handed it to me, saying, "All right, you keep it until we find the real owner. It probably belongs to the Girl Scouts."

I folded it and tucked it into my left hip pocket.

"Don't forget about the plastic clothesline —the brand-new one we just saw," Circus said, which I remembered was right that very minute stretched between two trees behind the tent and had a lot of women's different-colored clothes on it.

Things certainly were mixed up. The more we talked, the more tangled up everything seemed.

All this time, Little Jim had been hanging onto his brown manila envelope as though it was very important. I noticed he had a faraway expression in his eyes right then as if he was thinking about something a lot farther away than the cornfield we were in. Also, he didn't have any worries on his face, which I was pretty sure I had.

"Let's do a little more scouting around," Poetry suggested. "Let's send out a couple of spies to sneak up close to the tent to see what we can see or hear."

Big Jim shook his head a very savage no, saying, "You don't go sneaking around a tent where women or girls are camping! There's even a law against it. Remember what happened to that Peeping Tom they caught looking into a window in town last winter?"

"What's a Peeping Tom?" Dragonfly wanted to know.

And Big Jim, being the oldest one of the gang, explained it to all of us. When he got through, we made it a rule of the gang that not a one of us would ever be one.

That knocked out Poetry's scouting suggestion. We couldn't go spying around any tent or anyplace where there were women or girls.

Just that second, Dragonfly hissed the way he does when he has seen or heard something important. "*Psst!* Somebody's coming!"

We all looked and listened in every direction. Somebody *was* coming. Was it a man, or a boy, or a woman, or a girl? Who, or what?

I stooped low and looked down the corn row I was in. When I saw what I saw, I said softly to everybody, "It's a woman. She's wearing blue pants!"

That meant that six boys ought to scramble themselves out of there, which, on Big Jim's whispered orders, we did, hurrying like a covey of quail. But instead of fanning out in a lot of different directions as flushed quail do, we all followed Big Jim down his corn row, not stopping until we reached the bridge again.

"We'll go on over to the Tills' house right now," he said.

I noticed that Little Jim's hands were clasping tightly his manila envelope as he said, "Yeah, let's."

And away we went.

8

As much as I hated to leave the red boat and the green tent and the blue-dressed woman and the brown burlap bags with the water jugs in them, I was perfectly willing to go on to Big Bob Till's house. And, of course, Dragonfly was for some reason extraordinarily willing to get as far as possible from anybody who was a woman or a girl.

I was all set in my mind for whatever would happen when Big Bob and Big Jim saw each other. What *would* happen? I wondered.

I certainly was surprised when, just before we reached the wooden gate that led to the Tills' barnyard, I looked down at my hands and saw that somewhere on the way I had picked up a three-foot-long stick and was clasping it so tightly my knuckles were white. My eyebrows were down, my lips were pressed tightly together, and my jaw muscles were tense.

We looked around the barn first and called, "Hello," a few times, with nobody answering. Then we went inside, and out again, and through their orchard to the back door of their house.

Big Jim and Circus went onto the small roofless porch and knocked. And again nobody answered. "Hello," Big Jim called, and there wasn't any answer or any sound from inside the house.

"Hello, there," Big Jim called and knocked again. Still nobody answered.

While he was doing that, I noticed that Little Jim had his pencil out and was writing something on the manila envelope. My parents had taught me that it isn't polite to read over anybody's shoulder unless he invites you to, so I had a hard time seeing what he was writing, having to stand in front of him and crane my neck to read upside down. And—would you believe this?—that little guy had written:

Dear Bob,

Here's the Sunday school lesson book my mother promised your mother. Be sure to study all the questions so in case our teacher asks you any of them you will know the answers. We will stop for you at nine o'clock in the morning.

Your friend,
Little Jim Foote

I couldn't have read another line without getting a crick in my neck, but I remembered all of a sudden that it was to Little Jim's father, the township trustee, that Bob had been paroled. I saw Little Jim slip the envelope between the screen door and the unpainted, white-knobbed wooden door just as we were leaving. They had probably gone to town or somewhere, I thought.

In a little while we were back at the bridge again and across it. And, because it was Saturday and we were all supposed to get the chores done early so our parents could go to town, which most of them did on Saturday night, we separated, each one going to his own house. Even though Poetry was going to spend the night with me in the tent, he said he had to go home for a while, so I was all by myself when I got to the north road and turned left toward the Collins farm.

I moseyed lazily along, thinking and worrying and trying to figure out things. It just didn't seem possible that the gunnysack under the elderberry bushes last night had had a water jug in it instead of a watermelon. Even if it *was* possible, I didn't want to believe it. Of course, the woman or several women who lived in the forest green tent would have to have drinking and cooking water—even if they could have used the water from the creek to do their washing. Sugar Creek water wasn't good for drinking, even when it *wasn't* dog days.

A lot of ideas were piled up in my mind, but it seemed that one of them was on top, and it was: "If whoever had filled his or her water jugs at the spring, or at the Collinses' *other* iron pitcher pump, had done it at night, then whoever lived in the tent must be afraid to go to anybody's house in the daytime and ask for water. And if they were afraid to, why were they afraid?"

One other thing made me set my feet down

a little harder as they went *plop-plop* in the dusty road I was walking on. And that was: "Was the old car I had seen and heard in the lane last night the same as the gunmetal gray pickup that right this minute was parked beside the green tent?"

My mind was so busy with my thoughts that I was startled when I heard a car coming behind me. The driver gave what Dad would call a "courteous honk," which you are supposed to give when you want somebody to know you are behind them and don't want to scare the living daylights out of them.

A second later, the car had pulled up alongside and stopped, and I saw, sitting behind the steering wheel and wearing a watermelon-colored dress and sparkling glasses, a smiling, dark-haired lady about twenty years old.

"Hello, there!" she called in a friendly, musical voice. "I've been looking all over for you. Where have you been?"

Before I could answer, she had gone on to say, "You forgot to leave the map in the watermelon. The girls told me there was nothing in it."

"Map!" I asked with an exclamatory voice.

Interrogative sentences were galloping round and round in my mind. Then my thoughts made a dive for my left hip pocket.

My face must have had a question mark on it, because she said, "Don't you remember? You were going to make us a copy of the one you showed me. We wanted each of our girls to make her own map, using yours as a model, so that if any of them should get lost while they were here, they could easily find their way back to camp."

Before I could answer—not knowing what to say, anyway—she said with a laugh that was like the water in the Sugar Creek riffle above the spring, "I hardly recognized you, at first, with your haircut, and I see you've washed your face since yesterday, too. You certainly remind me of my little brother. His first name is Tom, too."

You could have knocked me over with a haircut, I was so surprised. All of a brain-whirling sudden, I knew who the watermelon thief was, and my mystery was practically solved. *Tom Till and I both had red hair and freckles, and each of us wore a striped shirt and blue denim jeans! The lady thought I was Little Tom Till!*

Just then somebody called from the direction of our farm, and it was Dad's thundery voice saying loud enough to be heard a quarter of a mile away, "Bill! Hurry up! It's time to start the chores!"

What little presence of mind I had told me not to answer, because it seemed I ought to let the smiling lady think I *was* Little Tom Till— for just a little while anyway. So I said to her, "That's Theodore Collins. He's calling his son to come and help him with the chores."

"You know the Collins family?" the voice that was still like the Sugar Creek riffle asked.

When I swallowed again and answered,

"Yes," she surprised me by saying, "I met your mother in town this afternoon. She seemed like a very nice person. You must be very proud of her."

"Uh—my mother? Which one? I mean— you *did*?"

"She and Mrs. Collins were together shopping. They invited our troop to church tomorrow. You go to Sunday school, I suppose?"

I got out a "Yes, ma'am," which she managed to hear, and before Theodore Collins called his son again about the undone chores, I said, "If you'll excuse me, I think I'll run over and see if I can stop him from having to call again. I think I know where his boy is."

My hip pocket seemed to have a fire in it that ought to be put out, so just before I started toward Dad to help put out a temper fire, which probably was ready to burn a hole in his hat, I handed to the lady the map Poetry and I had found last night in the watermelon at the spring, saying, "Is this what you wanted?"

She unfolded the "Eat more Eatmore" wrapper, spread out the map, and studied it. Her face lit up as she said, "Why, this is *good—very* good! It's even better than the one you showed me yesterday."

I liked her friendly voice and her smile so well that for a second I wished I was actually Little Tom Till himself.

Then she tossed another question at me. "This red X in the circle—does that represent any special location?"

"The red X?" I asked innocently. "Why, that's—that's where the green tent is pitched. I—it's straight across the creek from the mouth of the branch and just . . . uh . . . about fifty yards above where the current divides and one part goes down the north side of the island and the other the other."

She smiled and said thank you and added, "You do have a fine sense of humor, don't you?"

I wasn't sure *what* I had, but there was one thing I very much wanted to know. I felt I *had* to know it. What *did* the red letter X stand for? Of course, I knew the tent was there, but who lived in it and why? And why, if Tom had drawn this map for the Girl Scouts, *why* had he put the red X there?

I must have been frowning my worry and she saw it, because right away she added, "The girls will be intrigued by your story that an old witch is camping there, but I'm afraid instead of their wanting to stay away, they'll be more curious than ever."

Then my whole mind gasped. The lady in the watermelon-colored dress not only thought I was Little Tom Till, but that little rascal of a red-haired boy had told her there was a witch living in the tent and that the girls ought not to go anywhere near it. *What on earth!*

Just then Theodore Collins's thundery voice called again for his son, so I said, "I'd better go now," which I did. Away I went in a galloping hurry to let a reddish brown mustached, bushy-eyebrowed father know where his son really was—if he *was* his son.

I found Mr. Collins in a better humor than I expected. Panting and running fast like a boy who is late for school, I arrived at the barn door just as Dad came out with a pail of feed for our old brindle cow. She was standing at the pasture fence, looking at us with question marks on her ears as if wondering why her supper had come so early, but that it was all right with her.

"Why didn't you answer me when I called?" Dad asked.

I remembered an old joke our family had read in a magazine and which we had laughed over, so I said, "I didn't hear you the first two times."

"Bright boy," Dad answered.

I answered with another old joke, saying, "I'm so bright my parents call me 'son.'"

Dad grinned, and when I asked him how come we had to get the chores done so early, he explained, "There's a special prayer meeting for the men of the church. That's why your mother's in town now. She went in to get the shopping done this afternoon—she and Mrs. Till."

It was a good thing we *did* get the chores done early—a very good thing—because there were a lot of important other things that had to happen that day to make this story even more mysterious and to clear up some of the cloudy questions in my mind. Nearly everything had to happen before sundown. But, of course, I didn't know that at the time, or I'd have hurried even faster with my part of the chores.

I was up in our haymow alone, throwing down alfalfa hay when I looked out the east window and saw our car coming down the road. Mom was at the steering wheel, and Little Tom Till's mom with Charlotte Ann in her lap was in the front seat with her. Only a few minutes before, I had been thinking about Mrs. Till in a very special way, so when I saw her in the car with Mom, I got the strangest feeling.

Throwing down hay was something I always liked to do, because it is a man's job. Also there was something nice about being alone in a big, wide, alfalfa-smelling haymow, where a boy could think a boy's thoughts, talk to himself, whistle, even sing, and nobody could hear him.

Sometimes when I'm in the haymow, I climb up on the long, ax-hewn beam that stretches across the whole width of the barn from one side to the other and imagine myself to be Abraham Lincoln, who had split so many logs with an ax. I raise my voice and quote all of his Gettysburg Address, feeling fine while I am doing it, and important, and glad to be alive.

I always hated to stop when the last word was said and I would have to be Theodore Collins's son again, with years and years of growing yet to do before I would be a man.

Well, I had just said in my deepest, most dignified voice, ". . . That this nation under God may have a new birth of freedom, and that government of the people, by the people, and for the people, shall not perish from the earth." I was still standing and listening to my imaginary audience clap their hands, thinking about the part of my speech that said "all men are created equal" and also thinking of the Till family—old hook-nosed John Till himself; his oldest boy, Bob, and Little Tom, his other son, who wanted to be a good boy and was, part of the time. I was remembering the manila envelope that Little Jim had left at the Tills' back door and was thinking about Mrs. Till, who had such a hard time just to keep from being too discouraged to want to live . . .

Well, then is when I heard our car coming and saw Mom with Mrs. Till beside her. I quickly threw down another forkful of hay, hurried to the ladder, and climbed down, leaving Abraham Lincoln to look after himself and to get off the log the best way he could.

It seemed that Mom, by being a friend to Bob and Tom Till's mother, was helping to prove that "all men are created equal."

"All men are created equal" was still in my mind when I reached the bottom of the ladder. For some reason, though, it didn't seem right that red-haired, fiery-tempered, freckle-faced Little Tom Till was as equal as I was. We might look a lot alike to anybody who saw us dressed in the same kind of clothes, but I was *not* a watermelon thief and he was, I thought. And the first chance I got, I was going to prove to him that even though all men, boys especially, might be created equal, when one boy sneaked out into another boy's melon patch, stole a melon, and sold it to a Girl Scout troop, the other boy was equal to giving him a sound thrashing.

I was wondering whether I ought to tell Dad about what the Girl Scout leader had told me, when I heard Mom's voice calling from up near the walnut tree.

"Is Bill out there somewhere?"

I almost jumped out of my bare feet when I heard Dad answer her from just outside the barn door. "He's helping me with the chores!"

Mom called back to say that she wanted me to take care of Charlotte Ann while she drove Mrs. Till on home.

It wasn't easy, taking care of that wriggling, impatient little rascal of a sister. Whatever makes a little sister so hard to take care of anyway? And why do they always want to run away from you and get into dangerous situations the very second your back is turned?

I hadn't any sooner sat down in the big rope swing under the walnut tree, and had started to pump myself a little, than I heard Dad yelling from some direction or other. Actually, he was way up at the pignut tree—and how in the world did he get that far away so quick? He was yelling for me to "run quick and get Charlotte Ann away from Old Red Addie's fence."

I swung out of the swing in a hurry, for my eyes told me that my brown-haired sister was not only near the hog lot fence but was trying to crawl through it to get inside. Charlotte Ann wasn't afraid of a single animal on our farm—not even one.

I scattered our seventy-eight hens in even more directions than that as I flew to Charlotte Ann's rescue. Mom would have a fit if I let Charlotte Ann get her clean dress soiled and her best shoes muddy in Red Addie's apartment house yard—especially if she decided the mud puddle was a good place to walk in, which she probably would.

I got there just in time. *Honestly! That child!* You can hardly do anything else when you are looking after her. Mom calls it baby-sitting when she asks me to take care of her, but it isn't! It's *baby-running*. You have to keep your eyes peeled every second, or you won't even have a little sister. She'll be gone in a flash, and you have to look all over for her—like the time she got lost in the woods, and a terrible tornado roared into our territory, and trees were uprooted and fell in every direction.

Well, after what seemed too long a time of baby-running, Mom got back from driving Mrs. Till home, and I went to the car to help her carry in the groceries and other things. And that's when we found a brown paper bag with oranges in it, which Mrs. Till had accidentally left on the floor in the back.

"Yes, that's hers," Mom said. "I'd better drive right back with it. Her doctor wants her to have fresh orange juice three times a day."

"It's almost time to start supper," Dad said, looking at his watch. He reminded Mom about the special prayer meeting for men at the church, then gave me a quick order. "Bill, you take your bike and ride over to the Tills' with these oranges while your mother starts supper."

And that's why I ran into a situation that gave me a chance to prove in several fast hair-raising adventures that Little Tom Till and I were actually created equal.

I also got to find out who the old witch who lived in the green tent really was—and also why she lived there.

9

When I knocked at Mrs. Till's back screen door, she was in the kitchen, ironing something with an old-fashioned iron. I could see it was a pair of Tom's old, many-times-patched pants.

As soon as I'd given her the oranges and she had thanked me, she said, "You have such a nice mother, Bill. *Such* a nice mother."

I shifted from one bare foot to the other, swallowed something in my throat that hadn't been there a second before, and wished I could think of something polite to say. I couldn't at first, then managed to think of saying, "Tom has a nice mother, too."

I noticed Little Jim's brown envelope, with his awkward handwriting on it, lying on the other end of the ironing board. She'd probably read it, I thought. Then I got a little mixed up in my mind and was sorry for it afterward.

"*Bob's* got a nice mother, too," I said. I knew she knew *I* was thinking, *How could such a nice mother have two boys, one of which was a good boy and the other was a juvenile delinquent?*

There were tears in her eyes. She looked at me with a sad smile and answered, "I love them both—and someday God will answer my prayers for them."

I forgot for a minute that I had actually been thinking Tom was just as bad as his very bad big brother, Bob, because he had stolen my watermelon.

"Where's Tom now?" I asked.

She said, "I think he's down along the creek somewhere. If you see him or Bob on your way home, tell them it's chore time."

She thanked me again for the oranges, and I swung onto my bike and pedaled through their barnyard, out their open gate, and on toward the creek.

At the bridge I stopped, looked downstream again at the green tent, and, without even straining my eyes, I caught a fleeting glimpse of a boy just my size, wearing a gray-and-maroon-striped T-shirt. He was at the edge of the cornfield behind the green tent and close to the clothesline, which had on it women's different-colored clothes.

"Right now, Bill Collins," I heard my harsh voice saying to me through my gritted teeth, "right *now*, you're going to find out what is what and why. *Right now!*"

I was down the embankment and under the bridge in a hurry, then out in the cornfield, scooting along like one of Circus's dad's hounds trailing a cottontail—except that my voice was quiet.

Closer and closer I came to the place where I had last seen Tom Till, shading my eyes to see what I could see.

Right then I heard a whirlwind of flying

feet coming in my direction straight down the corn row I was stooped over in. In only a few fast-flying seconds, whoever was coming would be storming right into the middle of where I was. And if they didn't happen to see me and I didn't get out of the way, they'd bowl me over like a quarterback getting tackled in a football game.

There were sounds other than flying feet and the rustle of the corn blades, though. There was an angry man-sounding voice shouting, "Stop, you little rascal! Come back here with that! Do you hear me! I'll whip the daylights out of you if I ever catch you!"

There was also a small, half-scared-to-death voice yelling "Help! Help! *Help!*"

My muddled mind told me the small frightened voice was Tom Till's and the angry voice was his big brother Bob's—it sounded just like his—and that Bob was chasing his brother and if he caught up to him he would give him a licking within an inch of his life.

Even as I glimpsed Little Tom flying ahead of whoever was behind him, I noticed again that he was dressed the same way I was. His being dressed like that made us look like twins, although, of course, he looked more like *me* than I did *him*, which means he was a better-looking boy than I would have been if I had looked like *him*.

For some reason, when I realized that Tom was crying and running to get away from having to take a licking, in spite of the fact that I thought he was a watermelon thief, it seemed I ought to do something to save him.

Closer and closer and faster and faster those flying feet came storming toward me. Then, without warning, Tom swerved to the left and dashed down another corn row. At the same time, part of Abraham Lincoln's Gettysburg Address came to life in my mind, and I knew I was really going to do something quick to help save him.

A thought came lightning fast into my mind. I was dressed exactly like Tom, my hair was red like his, and we were the same height. From behind, we would look so much alike that whoever was chasing him wouldn't know the difference.

I glimpsed Bob coming and waited only until I felt sure he had seen me. Then, like a young deer, I started on a fast gallop down the same corn row. I was sure I could run faster than Tom, because I had beaten him in a few races, and it would be quite a while before Bob could catch up with me. When he did catch up, he'd stop stock-still and stare, and Tom would be safe—for a while anyway.

Well, the chase was on, and I was scooting down the corn row like a cottontail, running and panting and grinning to myself to think what a clever trick I was playing.

But that big lummox Bob seemed to be gaining on me. Within a few minutes he would have me, if I didn't run faster.

Faster! my excited mind ordered me. But I

quickly realized I couldn't save myself by just being fast. I'd have to be smart too, like a cottontail outsmarting a hound.

Remembering how cottontails disappear into a thicket if they can, then circle and go right back to where they were before, I turned left, as Little Tom had done, and raced madly back toward the tent and the creek and the plastic clothesline.

It wasn't a good idea. Bob heard me, or saw me, or something. I hadn't any sooner shot out into the open and dashed between a pair of brown pants and a lady's pink dress hanging on the line than I heard panting and flying feet behind me and knew I would have to be even smarter than a cottontail.

"You dumb bunny!" a savage voice yelled at me. "I'll make short work of you. Stop, you little thief! *Stop!*"

Right then was when my world turned upside down. *That fierce, very angry voice yelling at me was not the voice of Big Bob Till, but of somebody else!*

And I realized that it was somebody who, if he caught up with me, might not know that I *wasn't* Tom Till, and I would get one of the worst thrashings a boy ever got. *What,* I asked myself, as I panted and dodged and sweated and grunted and hurried and worried, *what will happen to me?*

I made a dive around the tent, planning to dart into the path that went through the forest of giant ragweeds to the bridge.

At the bridge I would rush up the incline on the other side and gallop across. As soon as I got across the bridge, I'd leap over the rail fence, hurry through the woods to the spring, get onto the path made by barefoot boys' feet, and in only a little while after that I'd be across the road from our mailbox and would be safe.

I took a fleeting glance over my shoulder to see who was chasing me, and—can you believe this?—my pursuer was not only not Bob Till but wasn't a boy at all. Instead he was a *woman* wearing brown pants and a woman's hat!

Boy oh boy, was I ever in the middle of a situation!

In that quick over-the-shoulder glance I noticed that her hat was straw-colored and looked a lot like the kind Little Jim's mom wears to church. Even in that quarter of a second I was seeing her over my shoulder, I saw that the hat was also the same color as the ripe wheat on Big Jim's dad's farm and that there were several heads of wheat slanted across its left side instead of a feather as lots of women's hats have on them.

What on earth! Why was I, Bill Collins, a husky, hardworking farm boy with muscles like those of the Village Blacksmith—"as strong as iron bands"—running from one helpless woman, just *one?*

But I hardly had time even to wonder what on earth, because in that fleeting glance my eyes had seen something else. I'd seen Little Tom Till storm out of the cornfield behind the forest green tent, shoot like a blue-jeaned arrow toward the tent opening, and disappear inside.

Glancing over my shoulder like that was one of the worst things I could have done. I had seen one red-haired boy dashing into a tent, and I knew where *he* was right that very second, but I didn't know where I, myself, was. When my eyes got back to the path I was supposed to be running in, I wasn't running in it at all. I had swerved aside, stumbled over a log, and now was making a head-over-heels tumble in the direction of the creek.

If the red boat hadn't been there, I'd have landed in the water. Instead, I fell sprawling into the boat—that is, that's where I *finally* landed when I came to a stop after rolling down the incline.

Looking up from my upside-down position, I saw the woman. Her face was hard and had an angry scowl on it. I realized with a gasp that in a minute she would be down the slope herself and I would be caught in what I could see were very large, very strong hands. Even though I was saving Tom Till from getting the daylights whaled out of him, I probably would get the *double*-daylights thrashed out of me.

If it had been winter and Sugar Creek frozen over, I could have leaped out of the boat and raced across the ice to the other side, but there isn't a boy in the world who can run or walk on water in the summertime. There was only one way for me to escape that fierce-faced woman, who in another few jiffies would be down that incline herself and into the boat and have me in her clutches.

Quick as a flash I was up and in the prow of the boat, unfastening the guy rope. Then, with one foot in the boat and the other against the bank, I gave the boat a hard shove, and out I shot into the stream.

"You come back here, you—you little red-headed rascal!" the woman's gruff, angry voice demanded.

I was in such a worried hurry to save myself that for the moment I had forgotten Tom Till. But then, what to my wondering ears should come sailing out over the water but Tom's own excited voice, calling, "Hey! Wait for me! *Wait!*"

Tom's high-pitched voice coming from behind her must have astonished the scowling woman. She turned her head quick in the direction of the tent, and her eyes landed on Tom, who was waving at me and yelling and running toward the creek, looking exactly like me in his blue jeans and maroon-and-gray-striped T-shirt.

She must have thought she was seeing double or that there were two of me. I was out in the nervous water in her red rowboat, floating downstream toward the Sugar Creek island. But I was also on dry land, running like a deer toward the creek, waving my arms and yelling to me in the boat to "Wait for me!"

The situation certainly couldn't have made sense to her. For a moment she just stood still and stared, while Tom scurried down the shore to a place ahead of me where there was a little open space. Then he half climbed and half skidded down the embankment, plunged into the water, and came *splashety-sizzle* toward the boat.

It was then that I noticed he was carrying something, which was making it hard for him to make fast progress. If my mind had had a voice, I think I could have heard it screaming an exclamatory sentence: *He's got another water jug with a burlap bag wrapped around it! What on earth!*

The woman wearing the straw hat with the little bundle of imitation wheat straw across its right side started on a fast run toward the place where Tom had plunged in, as though she was going to splash in after him and try to get to the boat first or else to stop him.

But in almost less than no time, Tom had hoisted his water jug over the gunwale and set it down into the boat at my feet. Then he swung himself alongside and climbed in over the stern, which is the way to climb into a boat without upsetting it.

"Hurry!" Tom Till panted to me. "Let's get across to the other side!"

I didn't know why he had been running, but I figured he would tell me as soon as he could—that is, if he wanted to. Besides, I was in a hurry to get across myself.

I reached for the oars, and that's when I got one of the most startling surprises of my life.

There weren't any oars in the boat—not even one! Not even a board to use for a paddle! All there was in the boat was a water jug with burlap bags wrapped around it, one very wet red-haired, blue-jeaned, maroon-and-gray T-shirted boy, and one *dry* one. And all the time our boat was drifting farther downstream toward the island.

In fact, right that very minute, the boat, which I had discovered was an aluminum boat painted red and was very light, was caught in the swift current where the creek divides and half of its current goes down one side of the island and the other half down the other side. There wasn't a thing we could do to stop ourselves from going one way or the other.

Swooshety-swirlety-swishety! Also *hiss-ety!* Those half-angry waters took hold of our boat, and away we went down the north channel between the island and the shore.

We weren't in any actual danger as far as the water was concerned. It was a safe boat. And after a while we'd probably drift close enough to an overhanging willow or other tree, and we could catch hold, swing ourselves out, and climb to safety—or to the shore anyway.

But we *were* in danger for another reason.

That woman wasn't going to let us get away as easily as that. I saw her begin to race down the shore after us, yelling for us to stop, which we couldn't.

"What's she so mad about, anyway?" I asked Little Tom Till.

His answer astonished me so much I almost lost my balance and fell out of the boat: "There's hundreds and hundreds of dollars in this water jug. It's the stolen money from the supermarket!"

Boy oh *boy!* No wonder there was a tornado in that woman's mind! And no wonder she didn't want two redheaded boys in blue jeans and gray-and-maroon-striped shirts in a rowboat to get away!

"She's sure mad as a hornet!" I said to Tom when, like a volley of rifle and shotgun shots, a splattering of very angry, very filthy words fell thick and fast all around on us and on our ears from the woman's very angry, very harsh man-sounding voice.

"She's not a *she,*" Little Tom Till answered. "She's a *he.* He's been hiding out in the tent pretending to be a woman, wearing women's clothes and earrings and hats and using fancy perfumes and stuff."

Every second, the fast current was swirling us downstream closer and closer to an over-hanging elm, one that had fallen into the water from the last Sugar Creek storm. Its top extended almost all the way across the channel from the north shore to the island. I could see that our boat was going to crash into its leafy branches and we'd be stopped.

I also knew that if we could manage to steer around the tree's top, we'd be safe for quite a while, because a thicket came all the way down to the water's edge over there. And if the fierce-faced woman—man—wanted to follow us any farther, he would have to leave the shore and run along the edge of the cornfield for maybe fifty yards before he could get back to the creek again.

If only we had even *one* oar, we could steer the boat near the island where there was open water. We could miss the fallen elm's bushy top and—

But then, all of a sudden we went crashing into the branches, and there we stopped!

That was when Little Tom Till proved that he had been created as equal as I had and maybe even more so. The very second we struck the tree, he scrambled to his feet, grabbing up the jug and the coil of clothesline that was fastened to it and yelling to me, "Come on! Let's get onto the island!"

It certainly was a bright idea. When our boat hit the tree, the current had whirled it around, and one end struck the sandy bank of the island and *stuck* against it. All we had to do was to use the boat as an aluminum-floored bridge, which in an awkward hurry we did. In a minute we were across and out and clambering up the rugged shore of the island into its thicket of willows and tall weeds and wild shrubbery.

"We're straight across from the sycamore tree and the cave!" Little Tom Till cried. "If we can get across the channel on the other side of the island, and into the cave, and go through it to Old Man Paddler's cabin, we'll be safe. Bob's up there helping him cut wood this afternoon—only he's mad at me about something."

The trouble was, the boat that had made such a nice bridge for us to cross on would make the same kind of aluminum-floored bridge for the woman—the man, I mean. He could climb out onto the elm's horizontal trunk, drop down into the boat, and get across as quick as anything.

Even as I scrambled up the bank behind my gray-and-maroon-shirted friend, I glanced over my shoulder and saw the brown pants with the woman in them—the man, I mean—on the trunk of the tree, working his way along through the branches toward the boat. In another second he would drop down into it, and in another he would be across and onto the island, racing after us.

Soon, the chase was on again—a wild-running, scared, barefoot-boys' race ahead of a short-tempered thief dressed in women's pants and wearing a woman's straw-colored hat. We dodged our way across that island, which was just a thicket of willow and wild shrubbery with here and there a larger tree and dozens of little craters hollowed out by the floodwaters that went racing across it nearly every spring. Banked against nearly every larger tree trunk were piles of driftwood and cornstalks and other stuff the creek had carried from different farmers' fields farther upstream and deposited there.

I guess I never had realized what a jungle that island was. I had been on it many a time when I was just monkeying around, looking for shells or studying birds with my binoculars. Once in a while at night in the spring or summer when it was bullfrog season, we would wade in the weedy water along the edge of the riffles with lanterns and flashlights, looking for the giant-sized brown and dark green monsters whose eyes in the light were like the headlights of toy automobiles. Bullfrogs, as you probably know, have long hind legs with bulging muscles, which, when they are skinned, are snow-white. When Mom fries them, they taste even better than fried chicken.

But such a *wilderness!* And so many rough-edged rocks for a boy's bare feet to get cut or bruised on, so many briers to scratch him, and so many branches to fly back and switch him in the face when another boy has just gone hurrying through ahead of him.

If we had been running from a real woman, or if only he had been wearing a dress instead of pants, he wouldn't have been able to take such long steps. And there would have been the chance he might get the skirt caught on a branch or a brier and be slowed down while we dodged our way ahead of him in our mad race to the other side.

"We're almost there!" Tom Till cried, panting hard from carrying the jug as well as himself.

I could see the other side of the island now and the nervous, excited water in the riffle racing between the island and the other shore. I could see the sycamore tree at the top of the bank and the mouth of the cave just beyond.

Another few seconds and we would be there, out in the fast current on our way to safety. It had been a terribly exciting race, I tell you, with Tom not letting me help carry the jug at all.

"It's not heavy," he panted. "It's made out of plastic, and it's as light as a feather. The money in it is in little rolls with rubber bands around them. I saw him stuff 'em in myself."

There were about a million questions I wanted to ask Tom, such as, How come he knew the woman was a man? How'd he find out about the money in the first place? And there were several other things that my mind was as curious as a cat's to know.

And then, all of a sudden, we burst out into the open at the water's edge.

Our pursuer was close behind, still panting and cursing and demanding that we stop. And I learned something else from that fierce-voiced villain when he yelled at Tom, "You little rascal! I'll catch you and your brother both, if it's the last thing I ever do. He's broken into his last supermarket!"

That was one of the saddest, most astonishing things I had ever heard. It startled me into thinking of a lot of other questions: Had Bob Till himself broken into the Sugar Creek supermarket last week? Was the man in women's clothes maybe a detective or secret agent who had been camping out along the creek, watching Bob's movements—his and Tom's?

Things were all mixed up even worse than ever.

For a minute, though, my watermelon mystery wasn't important.

Quick as a firefly's flash, Tom, holding onto the jug's handle with one hand, plunged into the fast riffle without even bothering to look or to ask me where the water was the most shallow. A second later he was up to his waist and losing his balance and falling. Up he struggled, and down he went, sputtering and wallowing along, with me doing the same thing beside him.

And then suddenly Tom let out a scared cry, "Help! H–e–e–elp!" as he lost his balance again and went down—*really* down. The coil of rope in his hand flew like a lasso straight toward me. At that minute I was quite a few yards from him, but part of the clothesline caught around my upraised hand with which I was trying to balance myself. The line tightened as Tom went down, still holding onto the jug's handle. And then down I went myself, like a steer at a rodeo, the water sweeping me off my feet.

And there we both were, struggling in the racing current—two red-haired boys, one on either end of a brand-new plastic clothesline.

Even as I went down I saw the willows on the island open up, and the maddest-faced man I ever saw in my life came rushing toward us. I also saw a puzzled expression on his face as if he was wondering, *What on earth?* Which one of us was Tom, and which was me, and which of us had the water jug with the money in it?

Just that second also, his woman's hat caught on a branch. Off it came, and off with it came a wig of reddish brown hair, and I noticed the man had a very short haircut.

But the woman was an honest-to-goodness man, all right. Actually he was a *boy,* maybe about as old as Bob Till himself. He had dirt smudges on his cheeks as if he had fallen down a few times in his mad race across the island after us. He was panting and gasping, and his woman's blouse was torn at the neck.

Tom and I must have looked strange to her too—*him,* I mean. I was like a calf on the end of a lasso, and Tom, now fifteen feet from me, with the jug in one hand, was struggling to stay on his feet, because I was downstream farther than he was and was being sucked along with the current while my feet fought for the pebbly bottom.

Then the mean-faced boy seemed to make up his mind who was who and what was what and what he ought to do about it. He rushed out into the water and with a series of fast lunges went straight for Tom, who began to make even faster lunges toward the other shore and the sycamore tree.

"Run! Swim! Hurry!" I yelled in a sputtering voice, which Tom couldn't do because right that second his feet shot out from under him and he went down again *kerflopety-splash-splash!*

I knew I could never wade back against the swift current to get to him in time to help. I'd have to get to the other shore *quick,* race along the bank to a place above him, and hurry out to where he was. I started to do that, but then *I* got stopped.

The current was stronger near the other shore and the water deeper. My feet were sucked out from under me. Again I went down. As I was pulled under, I felt the end of the rope still wrapped around my hand. With my hardly knowing it, I was holding onto that rope for dear life.

And right that second the bully caught up with Tom. He made a lunge with his right arm for the jug. He seized Tom with the other, and there was a wild wrestling match with curses and flying water and fast-flying arms. It looked as if Tom was going to get the living daylights licked out of him for sure.

Tom was trying to fight back but couldn't with only one hand and because of the swift current. He was as helpless as Marybelle Elizabeth in a chicken yard fight with Cleopatra.

Right then is when I remembered something important. I remembered that when a bevy of furious girls was beating up on Dragonfly at the spring, I had screamed bloody murder, given several wild loon calls, bellowed like a bull, and made a lot of other terrifying bird and animal noises, and it had saved Dragonfly.

Before I knew I was going to do it, I was yelling and screaming every savage sound I could think of in the direction of the one-sided fight, crying for help at the same time, hoping some of the gang might be somewhere in the neighborhood and hear.

And that's when I heard Big Bob Till's voice answer from the sycamore tree side of the channel. A second later he was standing in the black mouth of the cave. He held his hand up to his eyes, shading them as if he had been in the dark quite a while and the afternoon sunlight was too bright for them.

Then he seemed to see his little red-haired brother getting a licking within an inch of his life by a big bully. And *that* is when Bob Till, the fiercest fighter in all Sugar Creek territory, except for maybe Big Jim, came to life. It was like the cave was a bow and Bob was a two-legged arrow being shot by a giant as big as the one in "Jack and the Beanstalk."

I lost my balance then and went under. The rope in my hand went taut, the other end was torn from Tom's grasp, and the water jug, like a jug-shaped balloon wrapped in burlap, plopped to the surface and came on a fast downstream float toward *me.*

All I could see for a minute was Tom defending himself like a savage little tiger and Big Bob Till shooting through the air like a man from a flying trapeze. He leaped from the high bank out across ten feet of air, down and out toward where Tom was in the clutches of the thief. And then I was fighting to save myself from drowning, because I was in water over my head.

But my right hand still clung to the rope on the other end of which was the floating, plunging water jug with stolen supermarket money in it.

10

Before another second could pass, Bob Till landed feetfirst in the swift current and was storming his way through the six or seven feet of open water toward where his little brother, Tom, was holding on for dear life to the very same powerful-muscled overgrown man-sized boy who, a little while before, was wrestling with him, trying to get the water jug away from him. That little guy *really* knew what he was doing.

"Oh no, you don't! You great big bully!" Tom cried. "You don't get away so easy. Come on, Bob! It's him—the thief! Help! Help! *Help!*"

And Bob helped.

Talk about a fierce, fast fistfight. That was one of the fiercest, fastest ones I ever saw or heard. I really mean *heard,* in spite of my own battle to keep myself from losing my balance again in the deep, swift water I was in. If the rock bass and minnows and redhorse and other fish that were down in the water some- where had been watching that water fight, they'd probably have wondered what on earth.

Wham! Biff! Sock! Wham—wham—wham! Splash! Splash! Double-whammety! Pow!

"You great big lummox!" Bob yelled at his

opponent. "You *will* try to drown my little brother, will you! I'll teach you!"

The thief staggered backward in the water, his hands and arms waving fast in a lot of directions as he tried to steady himself. Then he struck the water and went under.

Bob seemed to know he had his man licked. He quickly turned to his little brother and half sobbed to him, "You poor little guy, fighting that big bully all by yourself!"

"Big Bully," as Bob had just called the fierce-faced thief—who wasn't a man at all and certainly wasn't a woman but was a powerful-muscled boy the size of Big Jim—came up from under the water with a bounce, like a cork plopping back up after you've pushed it under. He was sputtering and shaking his head and struggling to keep his balance in the rapids.

Then, spying the water jug floating on the surface down near where I was, he started on a fast half-run half-swim toward it and me.

One reason the jug hadn't already floated far beyond me was that the other end of the rope was still wrapped around one of my hands, and I was still holding on for dear life. The other reason was that the middle of the rope, which was down under the water, was tangled up with and wrapped around the bully's legs. I knew that for sure when I felt the rope tighten around my arm and felt myself being jerked off balance. And then down I went again.

It certainly wasn't any time to be thinking funny thoughts right then—not with all the dangerous excitement I was in and might not get out of without getting badly hurt. But a ridiculous idea popped into my mind and was: *I'm like a cowboy at a Sugar Creek rodeo. I've just lassoed a wild steer, and my bronco has just thrown me off into a racing riffle, but I'm going to hold onto him!*

Grunt and groan and puff and sputter and yell and scream and tremble with excitement and hold on tight and fight and just about everything else you can think of—we four were almost in a struggle for life.

I don't know how many times I lost my balance and went under or how many times I thought the thief was going to get the water jug away from us and get away.

And then all of a sudden, right in the middle of everything, I saw Bob's powerful right arm swing in a long, wide arc. And the fist on the other end of it caught the tough guy on the jaw. This time he went down and stayed down, and that part of the struggle was over.

I say *that* part was over. We had another and a harder job on our hands, and that was to save the bully from drowning, because Bob's experienced fist had knocked him completely out.

I saw the scared expression on Bob's face the very minute I heard his frightened words come crying out of his mouth: "I–I–I've *killed* him! What'll we do *now!*"

"Keep his head above water!" I yelled back. "He can't drown as long as his head is above water!"

Bob made a lunge for the big boy, clasped him the best way he could, and began to struggle with him toward the sycamore tree side of the channel. Little Tom and I struggled along beside and behind him, bringing the water jug filled with money.

It was just as it says in the Bible, which our minister is always quoting—and also my parents—where the words are: *"Be sure your sin will find you out."* That was what the thief's sins had done. The very rope he had stolen, along with the money, had accidentally lassoed his feet, making it possible for us to capture him.

The two gunnysacks that had been wrapped around the water jug came in handy, too. We unwrapped them from around the jug and spread them out on the ground. Then we cut two poles, using Bob's ax with which he had been helping Old Man Paddler. We slipped the sacks over the ends, making a hole in each of the closed corners, and we had one of the finest stretchers you ever saw. Then we used it to carry our prisoner from the sycamore tree to the toolshed in the woods behind Poetry's dad's barn.

Bob carried one end of the litter and Little Tom and I the other. Boy oh boy, did we ever feel proud, even though we were worried some because our prisoner was still unconscious. We knew he wasn't drowned, because he was breathing all right, but he was as pale as a sheet of gray writing paper.

Little Tom puffed out his story to me as we

struggled and grunted along. I helped with the story as much as I could by asking questions that had been worrying me for quite a while.

"How did you know he was the supermarket thief?" I asked him.

He said, "I didn't, at first. I wanted to make a lot of money to get a present for Mother's birthday tomorrow, so I thought up the idea of selling a map to the Girl Scouts—so the girls could draw a map apiece like we do when we go on our up-North vacations. The green lady worked out a scheme for me to leave the map in the big watermelon they had in the spring." Tom's face was as innocent as a lamb while he was puffing out his story to me.

"Then what?" I asked.

He said, "When I saw the melon—how big it was, and how pretty, as big and as pretty as your Ida—I got a sinking feeling in my stomach, wondering where they got it and if it might be yours. So I scooted up the hill and hurried to your garden to find out. I was feeling fine when I saw Ida was still there. I beat it back to the spring, plugged the melon like I promised I would, put my map inside, and went home."

"But how—" I began, still wondering how come he knew our prisoner was the supermarket thief.

He cut in on me, adding, "I didn't know till this afternoon. I saw all the women's clothes on the line behind the tent, so I thought there was a woman from somewhere camping in the tent.

I gathered a dozen eggs and went down to see if I could sell them to her. I was kind of scared because of being afraid of strange women and girls, so I sneaked up on the cornfield side and accidentally saw her doing it. That's how I found out."

"Saw her doing what?" Bob asked.

Tom answered, "She was rolling paper money into small rolls and stuffing them into a jug—it looked like hundreds and hundreds of dollars. I was so scared I couldn't move. I don't know what kind of a noise I made, but she—he—heard me, jumped like he was shot, quick squeezed the last roll of money into the jug, shoved it behind a suitcase, and yelled at me, 'What do you want?'

"'That's an awful lot of money,' I said. 'Where'd you get it?' And that's when the chase started."

"But somebody *did* steal Ida," I said and wondered what Tom would say about that. "Somebody sneaked out into our garden last night and took her."

Right that second our prisoner regained consciousness, opened his eyes. He began to struggle to get his hands and feet free and to sit up and get off our litter, which made us drop him *ker-plop* onto the ground.

We were busy for the next few minutes, but between grunts and groans and our thief's filthy language flying thick and fast against our ears, Tom managed to say, "Your prize melon's all right, and it's still not plugged. I saw it in the tent back over there by the cornfield, when I ran back for the jug."

And that's when our big bully of an overgrown boy growled into the middle of everything that was happening and said, "Maybe I took it myself. I was going to use a watermelon for a piggy bank instead of the water jug. Now are you satisfied?" And he started in twisting and fighting and trying to get away again and couldn't.

Several nights later, when Poetry and I were in our cots in the tent under the plum tree, while the drumming of the cicadas was so deafening we could hardly hear ourselves talk, we had one of the happiest times of our lives retelling each other everything that had happened.

"Who'd have dreamed that Muggs McGinnis would have been hiding out right in our territory?" he asked.

"Yeah," I answered across the moonlit four feet of space between our cots, "and imagine me being a good enough detective to capture him all by myself—Tom and Bob helping a little, of course."

When I finished saying such a boastful sentence, it seemed maybe I *had* been a pretty important hero. It felt fine to be one.

But Poetry spoiled my puffed-up feeling by saying, "It was Tom Till's keen mind that solved your mystery for you. That guy Muggs actually *was* getting his drinking water from your iron pitcher pump and from the spring with his jug. I, myself, thought of *that!*"

He yawned, rolled over, and sat up on the edge of his cot in the moonlight, looking like the shadow of a big fat grizzly. Then he yawned again and said, "I think I'll go get a drink. I can't seem to remember whether I got one the other night or not. Want to go along?"

I quickly was sitting up on the edge my own cot and saying, "Oh no, you don't!" I said it so loud it could have been heard inside the Collins downstairs bedroom.

And it was. A second later a thundery voice boomed out across the lawn from the window near the telephone, *"Will you boys be quiet out there? You'll wake up your mother, Bill. I've told you for the last time!"*

That is one of the most interesting sounds a boy ever hears around our farm.

Poetry was still thirsty, though, so I said, "I've had years of experience pumping that pump. I know how to do it without making it squeak. I'll get you a drink myself."

With that, I crept out of bed and moved out through the moonlight toward the pump platform.

That's when I heard Dad talking to somebody—to Mom, maybe, I thought—and I crept stealthily over to the living-room window to see if maybe he was saying anything about Poetry or me or about the exciting experiences we had had capturing Muggs McGinnis.

But Dad wasn't talking to Mom at all but to

somebody else. He was talking to the best Friend a boy ever had and the most important Person in the universe, the One who had made the stars and the sky and every wonderful thing in the whole boys' world. I'd heard Dad pray many a time at our dinner table and in prayer meeting at church but only once in a while when he was all by himself.

It seemed I ought not to be listening, but I couldn't move now or Dad would hear me, so I waited a while. And part of his kind of wonderful prayer was:

"Pour out Your love upon Muggs McGinnis and upon all the lost boys in the world. Help them to find out in some way that Christ loved them and poured out His blood upon the cross for the forgiveness of their sins.

"Bless our son, Bill, and our precious little curly-haired Charlotte Ann, so filled with play and mischief. And help Mother and me to bring them up to love You with their whole hearts and to always try to do what is right."

Mom must have been right there beside Dad, because when he finished, I heard her say, "Thank you, Theo. I can go to bed now without a worry in the world. I've given them all to Him."

And Dad answered, "I've decided you're not going to have even one hour of insomnia tonight—not even *one*."

Mom yawned and said while she was still doing it, "The way I feel now, I may not even have one minute."

I crept away then and moved out through the drumming of the cicadas and the cheeping of the crickets toward the moonlit iron pitcher pump, feeling fine inside and glad to be alive.